The Claus Family Album

*Stories of Santa Claus
and His Family*

by

Jonathan Claus

*Illustrated by
Joseph Bellofatto*

Illustrated by Joseph Bellofatto ©2002
Author - Jonathan Claus, et al ©2002

Paperback ISBN: 1-57646-645-0
Library of Congress Control Number: 2002095235

Quiet Vision Publishing
World Wide Web: http://www.quietvision.com
801-572-4018
Sandy, Utah

Printed and bound in the United States of America
Published - November, 2002

Table of Contents

I am Jonathan Claus

IT is always hard being the younger brother. Everyone expects you to be like your older brother. If your older brother likes to play basketball everyone expects you to play basketball, even when you would rather go skiing. But when your brother is going to be Santa Claus one day, basketball is only the start of your problems.

Being Santa's brother I am always hearing things like:

"You must be, like, a thousand years old," said one smart kid.

"Members of the Claus family live a long time but I am not even one hundred yet and Santa is only two years older." I told him.

"My Granddad said the 'Night before Christmas' is a hundred years old, so you are not right!" the kid retorted pronouncing each word emphatically.

"My brother is the eighty-second Santa Claus since Saint Nicholas, the first Santa Claus. Santa Claus is a job or actually a position of responsibility." I explained.

For a long time I tried to hide my true name, Jonathan Claus. But being a member of the Claus family, I could not hide the fact I was a Claus forever.

Why couldn't I hide? Well, in the Claus Family our hair starts turning white while we are still teenagers. And the enjoyment of making a child smile is too strong to overcome. And we all look a little like my brother.

As I got past 50, which is young for a Claus, my hair and beard were white and my size was large. As my beard grew, I started to notice strange things happening around me. I would go to the store and mothers would point me out to misbehaving children. Babies would stop crying and smile when they saw me. Young ones would peek at me from behind their fathers' legs.

The history and stories of my family and my brother, Santa Claus, needed to be told by a member of the Claus family. So with the help of Kori Aguirre-Amador, I am that historian and story teller.

I am proud to tell the world I am Jonathan Claus, the Younger Brother.

Mistaken Identity

Mistaken Identity

JUST going out in public is interesting when you have a famous brother. It is an adventure when you are Santa Claus' brother and you have the same white hair and beard. I am always being mistaken for my famous brother.

The barely heard whispers of "Do you know who that is?", "You better be good *you* know who that is.", "Santa!!", and many more echo all around. The echoes are louder and more frequent the closer Christmas comes each year. Many times I will go up to a child - even those 80 years old - and introduce myself. Everyone is pleased to meet Santa's younger brother.

I live near Snowbird, Utah with Laura Claus, the Claus Twins, Lily the Dalmatian, and The Mighty Quinn Mallory. One of my regular activities is to visit the St. Vincent de Paul Kitchen during lunch. There I spend my time talking and playing with the children. There I play with all the children: Destiny who is three, Joseph who is one, Anna Marie who is seventy, Mary, a kitchen worker, and Pinky her husband who are just big kids, Sam and Freddy, who never grew up, and others.

New children always stare and wonder: "Is it really him?"

I remember one cold, windy day during the 2002 Winter games. Laura and I decided to go to downtown Salt Lake City, Utah to see some of the exhibits. We took the light rail train along with what seemed to be the entire population of the world. The train cars were full with every seat taken and people standing in the aisles.

As we got on the train I saw the mothers and fathers pointing me out and heard the usual echoes. "See he is watching." "Better be good" and so on. Laura and I took a seat after a little while; we were lucky. A few stops later the usual crowd of people boarded. Just in front of us a tall seven year old stopped. Hiding behind an adult, she kept sneaking glances at me, eyes wide open.

After a short period of time and many stolen glances from her I asked, "Do you think you know me?"

Not even daring to speak, she shook her head yes and then stared at the floor.

"I am not him," I said. Hoping she would not be disappointed.

Jonathan Claus

"You're not!!!" she exclaimed with a very puzzled look on her face, "but you look just like Santa."

"Sorry I am not, I am his brother" and I gave her one of my cards:

𝔍𝔬𝔫𝔞𝔱𝔥𝔞𝔫 𝔠𝔩𝔞𝔲𝔰
𝔗𝔥𝔢 𝔜𝔬𝔲𝔫𝔤𝔢𝔯 𝔅𝔯𝔬𝔱𝔥𝔢𝔯

She stared at me, then at the card, then at me again, then at the card. Finally, after a full minute, she exclaimed "You have to meet my whole family!"

I must have met her whole family because there were 28 of them on the train: mother, father, grandparents, sisters, brothers, aunts, uncles, and cousins. Everyone in the family except the dog. I did heard his complete life history.

I still wonder who was more excited, the tall young girl with the extensive family or me.

That was only one of the many examples of the mistaken identity. My favorite happened when I was shopping for Christmas presents. Yes, that is right, shopping. The presents from the North Pole are for Santa to deliver on Christmas. I don't get presents for free to give to the Twins, my brother Santa and the rest of the family, I have to buy them as does Santa.

Now every Christmas Eve the Claus family gathers at my house to exchange presents — since my brother Santa works Christmas Day. We also do this the day after Christmas, everyone in the family loves to give and receive presents. Santa comes with his wife Joy, his whole family and a full team of reindeer. Many of the "elves" come but they are not really elves, they are the members of the Claus family that help Santa all year round. I remember the year he brought a kangaroo named Racer from his Australian team of "reindeer" but that is another story.

The reindeer come to play with Lily the Dalmatian and talk to The Mighty Quinn Mallory. It is well known that Santa's reindeer love to play. They love to play almost as much as dalmatians.

My mother, who is also Santa's mother, has passed on to me the job of buying the silly presents for the family. You know those gifts: the plastic snakes, tiny bows and arrows, trick marbles that wobble not roll and many others. One Christmas I found a tinsel wig for The Lizard, one of my nieces. This sent Lily the Dalmatian and Trea, the guide dog being raised by The Lizard, running for the door.

One Christmas Eve Eve (that is the day before Christmas Eve), the last store I visited was the dollar store. You know one of those stores where nothing costs more that a dollar. I picked up some chocolate, there is no such thing as too much chocolate on Christmas, some hard butterscotch candy, and some cherry cola. The next stop was the toy wall in the back of the store. There I found a hula hoop, foam squares with numbers on them to put on the floor, some toy whistles, puzzles, and enough kaleidoscopes for the Twins and their cousins.

Looking along the wall, I noticed out of the corner of my eye, a little girl about four or five years old with one of the largest frowns I have ever seen. I smiled at her but her frown grew even larger, so I went about my shopping.

As I walked about the store, the little girl followed me at a distance dragging her father by the hand. I stopped, she stopped. I walked, she walked. All the time wearing the large frown.

Finally it was time to check out and I was not surprised to see the little girl peeking out from behind her father's legs. He was right behind me in line.

I never like to see a child, large or small, frown. I also noticed that familiar look in her eyes, the one that said she thought I was my brother.

"Do you think you know me?" I asked gently.

The frown only deepened.

"Who do you think I am?" I asked wondering why the frown continued.

Then she said something which I did not understand. I looked at her, then at her father.

"She thinks you are Santa Claus," said her father.

"I am sorry," I said, "I am not Santa Claus. I am only his brother."

All of a sudden the frown disappeared and a huge smile appeared. A flood of questions came from the little girl.

"Is Santa really your bother?" "Do you know what I want for Christmas?" "Where is he now?" "Have you ever seen his reindeer?" "Do you make toys?" "Do you see him a lot?"

I seized on this last question before another could come out and answered, "I don't get to see him much this time of year."

"He's very busy," she said with a very almost adult look. I now realized she had thought I was Santa Claus and was buying her Christmas toys at the dollar store. Her special toy was clearly not there.

Jonathan Claus

"Do you know where he is this time of year?" I ventured.

The little girl turned slowly until she was faced due North, pointed and said emphatically;

"He's up there."

The First Santa Claus

The First Santa Claus

WHO is Santa Claus? Well that is a silly question, any four year old child can answer it. But did you know that there has been more than one Santa Claus? My brother, Tomás, is the eighty-second Santa since the first one.

However, before I explain about the many Santa Clauses, I will tell you about the first Santa Claus.

The very first Santa Claus lived in the fourth century after Christ. His name was Nicholas of Patara, which is a city in Lycia, Asia Minor. He was the bishop of Myra and was known for his good deeds. Actually he is so well known for his good deeds that he is considered a saint and has become known as Saint Nicholas.

Now Patara was just like any other city in the fourth century or today, there were goods things in it and there were bad things in it. One of the particularly bad things about that city was that many people were poor and those people would sell their children when they could not take care of them. Just about everyone in Patara knew this was wrong, but they did not know what they could do about it. And Nicholas did not know what to do about it either.

However, unlike all the other people in Patara, Nicholas was determined to do something. He did not really care what, just as long as he did something. Now, it took Nicholas some time to think of what exactly to do, and he ended up doing the simplest thing. He decided to simply give children some money and then their parents would be able to take care of their children and would not have to sell them.

"But how can you do this?" Nicholas' wife asked when he told her his plan, "How will you find enough money?"

Nicholas shrugged. "I'll find a way," he said.

"But how are you going to find a way?" his wife asked, "You're going to need to find money."

"I know," Nicholas said, "But I'll find a way somehow. I'll even find money too. Somehow."

"But how?" his wife asked once more.

Nicholas shrugged again. "It's a mystery."

Well, Nicholas set out that very day to find his way of helping the children. And, of course, that meant he had to find enough money to give to all the children who needed it. Now as you may have noticed, Nicholas had a tendency to solve things the simple way. Nicholas went from house to house of everyone he knew, and that was a lot of people since Nicholas was a fairly sociable fellow. And Nicholas asked everyone of those people how they would solve the difficulty he had come across. He asked them how they would come up with the money to help all the children who needed it.

The first person Nicholas asked really did not know how anyone could come up with that much money. He shrugged and said, "Sorry I can't solve the problem for you." He then dug into his pockets, "But here's a little bit of money for you," and he gave Nicholas a few coins.

Now this may not seem like a lot of money to you, but the next person Nicholas asked said and did the same thing. He said, "Sorry, but I don't have the faintest clue where you could come up with that kind of money, but here," he dug into his pockets and pulled out a handful of coins, "see what you can do with this."

Now the spare change of two people still did not amount to a whole lot of money, but I mentioned earlier that Nicholas was a fairly sociable fellow. Nicholas had always been a kind person and he was always doing good deeds for just about everyone he came across. And so, naturally, just about everyone remembered him for being so kind. And there was hardly anyone who could refuse to help Nicholas, and no one who could refuse helping after hearing how Nicholas wanted to find some money to help poor children.

So when Nicholas visited everyone he knew to ask for a solution, everyone he knew found himself wanting to help out somehow. So everyone Nicholas knew gave a little bit of their own money to him so he could help the children. And then a very odd thing happened, people who did not know Nicholas heard about how he was trying to help the children and so they gave a little bit of their money to help the children. And then people who did not even like Nicholas started giving him a little bit of their own money just so they would not be left out.

And while the spare change of two people did not amount to a whole lot, the spare change of the entire city of Patara amounted to a whole lot of money. Actually, it amounted to a small fortune, one just large enough to provide for all the poor children so they would not have to be sold.

Now it was December 6th. Nicholas mounted his horse and

started his journey through Patara. This is why you sometimes see pictures of Santa Claus riding a horse. At each house with a child that needed help, he placed a small bag of coins in each child's socks or shoes. He did this secretly, in the dark of the night. Have you ever found a few small coins in your Christmas stocking? Santa Claus still does this at a few houses. It is his way of remembering Nicholas.

Needless to say, Nicholas was quite happy with the result. A problem that no one thought would ever be solved, had just been solved. Actually, Nicholas was so happy with that result that he decided to do the same the next year. And it worked just as well, so he decided to do it again the year after that, and the year after that. Nicholas gave money to poor children for the rest of his life, but a funny thing happened between the first time he did this and the last time.

You see, after a few years of having enough money, parents stopped selling their children. Whenever they did not have enough money, Nicholas would give them the money. So after a time, no more children were being sold, and people forgot that they had ever sold their children. But Nicholas enjoyed giving out gifts so much that he did not want to give it up, so he decided to start giving out toys instead of money. After all, sometimes being happy is just as important, or more important, than having money.

And Nicholas thoroughly enjoyed giving out toys every year, he started looking forward to the day each year he would give out the toys. All of his family, including nieces, nephews, aunts, uncles, cousins, and children started helping all year to make toys for the special day. Nicholas would wait all year for that day, deciding what toys he would give, and which children deserved extra toys.

Saint Nicholas was the first Santa Claus. Even today in parts of the world Santa Claus is called Saint Nicholas and other names. I will call all of Saint Nicholas' successors Santa Claus even though that name is only about 200 years old. The name Santa Claus comes from the Dutch words Sant Nikolaas and a little confusion about how to pronounce them in English.

The family of Saint Nicholas, my family, is the Claus family. We still help Santa Claus with his yearly work. Designing toys, making toys, taking care of the reindeer, listening to children's Christmas Wish Lists, watching for naughty and nice children, and writing Christmas stories are among the many jobs of the Claus family every Christmas.

The first gifts from Saint Nicholas were delivered on December

Jonathan Claus

6th not on Christmas Day. In many parts of the world Saint Nicholas or Santa Claus still delivers his gifts on December 6th, his feast day, or on January 6th, the feast of the day the Magi delivered their gifts to the Christ Child.

After his death in 345, yes the first Santa Claus died, the Claus family continued the tradition of delivering gifts to children who believed in Saint Nicholas. The Claus Family's work of good cheer soon expanded beyond Patara over Asia Minor, to Europe, to the entire world. In some parts of the world the gifts are placed in shoes or stockings and in other parts under a Christmas tree.

So, "Who is Santa Claus?" is a very good question. He is the same person who every four year old knows, and he is my brother. He is the person who organizes and delivers millions of toys for millions of children every year. He is the person doing this job today, the current person in a long line of people from the Claus family dating back continuously to St. Nicholas in the 4th Century.

He is Santa Claus.

Choosing Santa

Choosing Santa

YOU have learned that there have been many Santa Clauses throughout history, and that all of these Santa Clauses were in the same family, the Claus Family. Now that you know all of this, you are probably wondering how the family chooses who will become Santa Claus. After all, you have to imagine, that every single Santa Claus, was once a child, just like you are or were. And that every single Santa Claus had brothers or sisters or cousins, and parents and aunts and uncles. In short, Santa Claus is almost just like a normal person. Almost.

There are, of course, some things that are decidedly different about Santa Claus. Santa Claus is always an incredibly nice and good natured person. Santa Claus also always loves children and loves toys. Santa Claus also has to be generous, after all, it takes a very generous person to give away all the toys that he has to give away every year.

Now, naturally, you wonder how do we choose who will be Santa Claus. And my answer will probably not satisfy you. The answer is, we always know. It is hard to explain, but I will do the best I can. You see, members of the Claus family do not compete to become Santa Claus, somehow, we just *know* who is going to be Santa Claus. From an early age the family knows he or she — yes, there has been more than one girl Santa Claus — was absolutely meant to be Santa Claus.

I figured the best example to use to explain this would be the case of my own brother, Tomás, who is of course as you know the current Santa Claus. Tomás is of course a Spanish name. In the sixteen and a half centuries since Saint Nicholas, the Claus family has spread all over the world. Members of the Claus Family come in every color and nationality you can think of.

From the time we were children, everyone knew that Tomás would grow up to be Santa Claus. Now Tomás was hardly the perfect child. Trust me, as his brother, especially as his younger brother, I know exactly what he was like as a child.

As you know, Tomás, Santa Claus, is my older brother, and if any of you have an older brother you know exactly what I am talking about. For those of you do not have an older brother, I will give you an example: baby-sitting. There always comes a time when the older brother or older sister is finally old and mature enough to baby-sit the younger sibling. And naturally enough, this happened in my family too, when Tomás was eleven and I was nine.

About this time, our parents decided that Tomás was old enough to watch me while they were away for the afternoon with Malcolm, who was four, and James, who was two. They decided that I was old enough not to get myself into serious trouble. By serious, it should be noted, I mean life-threatening. They trusted me not to get into any trouble that was life threatening to me or, more importantly, to anyone nearby. As you might have guessed, neither Tomás nor I were really up to the responsibility.

Naturally, the first thing that happened was Tomás began bossing me around, as so many older siblings are apt to do.

"You need to clean your room, Jonathan," Tomás stated no more than one second after our parents had left.

"Why?" I asked. After all, Tomás was only my older brother, I had no intention of doing anything he said, especially not after he had told me to do something.

"Because your toys are all over the floor," Tomás said, sounding very snotty as he did so, "and I said so."

"Are not," I said. Of course, you must understand that from my perspective my room looked perfectly fine. Now what it looked like from everyone else's point of view is quite a different matter.

"Are too," Tomás argued.

"You're not Mom," I said, "I don't have to do anything you say." And I did not intend to do anything he said. I intended to do all the things I had never dared do when our parents or a baby sitter was home.

"But I *will* be Santa Claus one day," Tomás said, you see, every-one already knew he was perfect for the job, and so Tomás knew too that everyone knew he was going to Santa Claus, "And if you don't pick up your room you'll get on the Permanent Naughty List. And then you'll never get presents ever again."

I was a little frightened by this, but I was not going to let Tomás know this. "There's no such thing," I said, "Uncle Liam doesn't have a Permanent Naughty List, it doesn't exist."

"Does so," Tomás said, "Uncle Liam just doesn't talk about it in front of you."

"Why not?" I asked, I was pretending to not believe him, but

Tomás being the older brother and being in charge at the time caused me to believe him just a little.

"Because it's a secret," Tomás whispered, "It's the deepest secret of Santa Claus. No Santa Claus ever lets it get out because they're all afraid it will scare the little kids."

I must admit, as an nine year old, the thought did scare me a little. But I would never let Tomás know that. I tried to act causal and said, "I don't believe you, I already know all the family secrets."

"OK," Tomás said, "If you really don't believe, you don't have to. But if you get on the Permanent Naughty List, you'll never, ever get any presents ever again.'

"Oh yeah," I said, I was starting to lose my temper by this time, "Well you're going to have to wait until you're Santa Claus to put me on the Permanent Naughty List, and you're going to be old by that time, you'll forget to put me on it."

"Santa Clauses remember everything," Tomás retorted, "How else do you think they all remember those Naughty and Nice Lists?"

"Aunt Florence types them all out for Uncle Liam every single year" I said, and it was true, Aunt Florence always had to have the computer print out the Naughty and Nice Lists for Uncle Liam.

Tomás had to think about his answer for a minute. "She just does that for everyone else," Tomás finally said, "You know, so all the toy companies will know how many toys they have to make and stuff."

Being nine years old, this explanation made sense to me, and I secretly believed in the Permanent Naughty List. "Oh yeah," I finally said, "Well I think the Permanent Naughty List is a stupid idea." Again, being nine years old, this was a perfectly understandable and well founded argument. And I walked off believing that I had won the argument.

And of course the first thing I did once I had left Tomás behind in the living room was go to my room and pick up all of the toys off my floor.

Now, for all of you out there worrying, there really is no such thing as a Permanent Naughty List. And by the time I figured that out, I was far to old to hold a grudge against Tomás, and, naturally, I felt very indignant about that, it would have been a great grudge.

But that is a perfect example of what the current Santa Claus, Tomás, was like as a kid. He was far from the perfect child, and for the longest time, I thought everyone else in the family was crazy for choosing him to be Santa Claus. It was not that I ever wanted to be Santa Claus myself, but, I just could not imagine Tomás as Santa Claus, it seemed like he was never nice or generous to me. Personally, I thought the rest of the family was losing it.

But I was wrong. By the time Tomás and I were finally adults, I realized that he had become a lot nicer and more generous than I remembered him being as a child. And to my surprise, Tomás has made a decent Santa Claus. So far.

The First Reindeer

J. Bellofatto ©2002

The First Reindeer

AS everyone knows, Santa Claus' sleigh is pulled by reindeer, well, except in Australia when he gives the reindeer a day off and has his sleigh pulled by a team of kangaroos. But for the most part, his sleigh is pulled by a team of nine reindeer.

However, the first Santa Claus did not have reindeer, in fact the first Santa Claus did not even know what a reindeer was since he lived in Asia Minor. Not even the second Santa Claus had reindeer, nor the third nor the fourth. The first Santa Claus to have reindeer was Joshua Claus, the ninth Santa Claus. Joshua lived in Lycia in Asia Minor, just like Saint Nicholas and all the Santa Clauses before him. Like all the Santas before him, Joshua was very well known. Everyone knew that he was Santa Claus. Everyone knew it was he who delivered the Christmas presents. But unlike all the other Santas before him, everyone knew where he lived.

Children would constantly come to his house, knock on his door, and give him their Christmas Lists in person. While this was all very cute, it posed quite a large problem for Joshua. At that time the Claus family had to make each and every present that was delivered on Christmas Day. Being constantly interrupted by children knocking on the door was making it hard for them to make all the toys they needed to before Christmas.

One day, after listening to a particularly long Christmas Wish List, Joshua reached a decision; he had to move. He needed time to make his gift list and his Naughty and Nice List. So as soon as a boy with a long list left he called all the family together to tell them.

"Who was at the door?" Joshua's daughter-in-law Denise asked as soon as everyone was gathered together.

"Another child with a Christmas List," Joshua sighed, "In fact it was the same boy who came last week to tell me his Christmas List, there were a few revisions."

"That's the fifth one today," Denise said.

"I couldn't get any toys made today," Joshua's brother Edgar complained, "because three kids snuck into the basement and I had to hide all the toys."

"And I couldn't make any progress on my Naughty and Nice List today because I had to listen to five Christmas Lists," Joshua said.

"Well," Sean, Denise's husband asked, "Is there anything we can do about it? Can we stop answering the door or something and board up the windows?"

"No," Joshua shook his head, "I can't just ignore the kids, it wouldn't be nice," he said. After all, Joshua was a very nice person and would never be rude to anyone, even if they did annoy him.

"And you can't board up the windows," Angelica, Santa's wife said firmly, "I just painted them and no one's going to ruin them."

"Then what are we going to do?" Marian, Joshua's niece, asked, "If we don't do something, we won't have half the toys we need for Christmas, and Uncle Joshua won't even know who's been naughty or who's been nice."

"We need to move," Joshua said firmly.

Everyone was shocked and silent for a minute. "Move," Angelica finally said, "We can't move, I just painted the windows and replaced the kitchen floor."

"It's either we move, or we board up the windows, and the front door," Joshua said firmly again.

And so it was decided, in order to keep Christmas going, the Claus family would have to move somewhere where children would not be able to find Santa very easily and where no one would be able to find the toys and ruin the surprise before Christmas. The only question was where could they move to? If they simply moved to another village, it would not be long until the people in that village figured who Joshua was and then the whole family would have to move again.

In the end, the Claus family decided to just move north, and to keep moving north until they found a spot where no one could find them. They moved north out of their village, past the next village, and the village after that. They moved north to where it was much, much colder than Lycia and to where the snow became so deep the Claus family could hardly move north anymore.

"Are we far enough north yet?" Marian asked.

Joshua shook his head and answered, "No. Look over there," he pointed to a group of people herding some animals into a pen, "There's still people around, we have to go where there are no people at all."

"But the snow's too deep," Marian, his niece, complained, "And I'm tired, I want to stop now."

"Let's stop for a little while," Edgar said, dropping the large of bag he had been carrying in the snow, "At least long enough for me to make a sleigh to carry all these toys in."

"But those people are going to figure out who we are soon," Joshua protested.

"We just need to stop long enough for Edgar to make a sleigh," Angelica said dropping her own bag in the snow.

Everyone else dropped their own bags, sat down and waited for Edgar to make a sleigh to carry all of the toy bags.

That is, everyone but Joshua, he was anxious to get to wherever they were going to so he could get back to working on his Naughty and Nice List. True, Christmas was still months away, but it takes almost a year for Santa Claus to put that list together, and he was already behind schedule. But even though, and he tried, he could not convince one single other member of the Claus family to continue. They all wanted Edgar to make that sleigh to carry all their bags, and they all refused to budge until it was made. And so, Joshua finally gave up and waited along with the others for Edgar to make that sleigh.

Edgar started working on the sleigh. Edgar was the best toy maker in the world, after all, he had to make the world's Christmas toys. He was also a very fast worker, and by the end of the day, he had half of the sleigh built. However, Joshua had been right about one thing, it did not take the people long to become curious about the Claus family. First it was the children, who came to watch Edgar build the sleigh, then they dragged their parents and grandparents to come and watch Edgar work on the sleigh.

"What is he building a sleigh for?" one child asked, tugging on Joshua's sleeve.

Joshua had been working on his Naughty and Nice List, but he just could not ignore the child's question, that would be rude. "So we can move north," Joshua answered, even though he was a very good natured person, he wished the child would go away. If he did not finish this list, he would not know who was naughty and who was nice. And if he did not know who was naughty and who was nice, he might deliver presents to the wrong children, and that would just not be fair.

"Why are you moving north?" the child asked, pulling on Joshua's sleeve some more.

"Because I need to finish this list," Joshua answered, "And my brother needs to make toys. And we need to have this done before Christmas, and we can't have anyone interrupting us."

The child tugged on Joshua's sleeve some more. "Who's going to pull the sleigh when he finishes it?" the child asked.

Joshua was about to answer, when he realized he did not know. He had never thought of that. He went over to Edgar who was busily putting the finishing touches on the sleigh. He tapped Edgar on the shoulder. "Who's going to the pull sleigh?" Joshua asked.

"Why..." Edgar paused, apparently he had not thought of who would pull the sleigh either, "Why I don't know. Do you want to pull it?"

Joshua shook his head, "It'll be too heavy with everyone's bags in it."

"Hmmm..." Edgar said, thinking, "It'll be too heavy for you to pull, or for me to pull. Actually, it's going to be too heavy for anyone to pull." Edgar set his tools down and sat himself down. Joshua sat down next to him, this was a bigger problem than either of them had thought they would encounter.

Joshua felt a tug on his sleeve, he looked to see the same child tugging on it. "Yes?" he asked.

"I know who can pull the sleigh," the child answered.

"You do?" Joshua asked, "Who can pull the sleigh?"

"Dasher and Dancer and Donner and Blixen and Comet and Cupid and Prancer and Vixen," the child answered. You may know there is a ninth reindeer, Rudolph, but how he joined the team is another story.

"Excuse me?" Joshua asked, "Who and what are they?"

"They're reindeer," the child said, "And they can pull anything, even a sleigh full of Santa Claus' toys."

"Reindeer," Edgar said thoughtfully, "Reindeer would work perfectly."

But Joshua was concerned with something else the child had said. "How do you know I'm Santa Claus?" he asked.

The child shrugged, "You look just like him."

After Edgar finished the sleigh, they hooked all eight of the reindeer the child had named to a harness to pull the sleigh. The reindeer pulled the sleigh, not only with all the bags of toys in it but with all the Claus family in it as well. They went north until they could go north no more, until they had reached the northernmost spot in the world, the North Pole. And there was no one there, no one to give their Wish Lists to Santa in person, no one to sneak into Edgar's workshop and take a peek at the toys. And the Claus family was able to work on Christmas in peace.

And when Christmas came, Joshua used the sleigh Edgar had made and the reindeer the child had given him to deliver the Christmas presents. Since that time every Santa Claus has lived at the North Pole until they retire to the Claus family's hidden tropical island. Every Santa since has used the very same sleigh Edgar had built. The descendants of the first eight reindeer and Rudolph still pull the sleigh every Christmas, except in Australia. And every reindeer today is called by their family name, Dasher and Dancer, Prancer and Vixen, Comet and Cupid, Donner and Blixen and Rudolph.

Which One Are You?

Which One Are You?

IN prior stories I have mentioned the Claus Twins, Stacy and Tracy, my daughters. This story occurs when they were younger, about twelve years old. They are now both in college. They also have an older brother, Sean, who is the father of the second set of Claus Twins, Dizzy and Tizzy. Dizzy is two and Tizzy is one, but this story is about Tracy and Stacy.

Stacy stands about medium height, with long, straight blond hair. Tracy is the same height, with curly brown hair and is one year younger than Stacy.

The Twins are identical. That is, they look just like each other, and everyone is always mistaking one for the other. It happens at school. It happens at work. It happens everywhere the Twins go. No one ever says "Hi, Stacy," or "How are you, Tracy?" Instead they always say "Which one are you?" Much to the annoyance of both of the Twins.

One day, which happened to be the last day of Chistmas vacation, the Twins became so annoyed with this situation that they decided to do something about it. Stacy had decided to cut her hair, her waist length golden blond hair.

"Cut your hair?" Tracy said, entirely shocked at the idea, "You can't do that."

"Why not?" Stacy answered, "Everyone is always mistaking me for you, and I'm sick of explaining that I have a Twin. If I cut my hair, we won't look alike any more."

"But your hair's so long," Tracy argued, after all, it was common knowledge that no one is allowed to cut long hair.

"But so's yours," Stacy protested, "You see, the problem is that we both have long hair, that's why we look alike."

"Great," Tracy rolled her eyes, "So I can be 'The One With The Long Hair' and you'll be 'The One With The Short Hair'. And they'll probably still get our names mixed up."

"Well it's better than 'Which One Are You?' I'm never going to answer that question again," Stacy stated defiantly. She handed Tracy a pair of scissors, "Here," she turned around and held her golden blond hair, which was in a long golden braid, out for Tracy, "start cutting."

Tracy took hold of the braid and scissors. She opened the scissors and held them by the hair. But she just couldn't cut. "Are you *sure* ?" she asked, "What if you miss your hair and want it back?"

Stacy held up a tube of glue. "Super Santa Glue," she stated, "See, we're going to keep my braid, then if I miss it, we can glue it back on."

Tracy took the tube of glue, it wasn't just any glue, it was *Super Santa Glue*. This glue was one of the many Claus family inventions of which only Santa and the Claus family knew about. And everyone knows, that unlike any other glue ever made, Super Santa Glue can glue anything together.

"OK," Tracy said positioning the scissors again to cut the braid, "Here it goes." Tracy shut her eyes and cut the braid off completely.

The next day the Twins went to school. Stacy was so confident that her new short hair would set her apart from Tracy that she didn't even bother to wear the opposite colour of clothes as they usually did. Stacy smiled all through breakfast, all through the bus ride, and smiled as she walked into the classroom holding her head high, displaying the newly cut hair.

"Hey," one of the Twins' friends, Marie, called running up to Stacy, "uh ... Which one are you?"

Stacy just stood rigid, looking at Marie. She closed her mouth tightly, you know, in that way that makes it clear that she does not mean to answer any time soon.

"Come on tell me," Marie begged, "you know I can't tell you two apart, no one can."

Stacy still refused to answer. She crossed her arms in front of her and pressed her lips even closer together.

"Um..." Marie said quietly to Tracy, "Is there a reason why she's not saying anything? Does she have laryngitis or something."

"It's something like that," Tracy answered quietly, "She refuses to ever answer that question again."

"Oh," Marie said, understanding, "What question? I don't ever ask any questions."

"Which one are you," Tracy answered.

"What do you mean which one am I?" Marie asked indignantly.

"No, that's the question she's refusing to answer," Tracy said beginning to become annoyed herself, "She's sick of everyone getting us mixed up."

"Oh," Marie said, understanding, "Then I won't ask anymore."

"Good," Tracy said. Maybe Stacy's new haircut was working after all.

"So..." Marie said to Tracy "Which one are you?"

"I thought you weren't going to ask anymore," Tracy said very annoyed now.

Marie looked confused. "Well, I wasn't going to ask *her* anymore, not you anymore," Marie tried to explain, but it just made everyone even more confused. "Unless you're her now, and you guys switched places or something. But if you're her, then where's you, 'cause I need to ask you which one you are so I know who you are. Got it?"

Needless to say, Tracy didn't get it. Even Stacy, who was trying her best to ignore Marie, could not help looking confused. "No," Tracy answered, "Do you get it?"

Marie looked confused for a minute. "No," she answered, shaking her head. Then apparently too confused to continue, she left with a dazed sort of look.

"I don't think she noticed your hair," Tracy said quietly to Stacy.

"Everyone else will," Stacy said, confidently.

The Twins took their seats, right next to each other as usual. Everyone else was slumped over their desks, either half asleep or all the way. But not Stacy, she was sitting up tall and constantly fixing and fiddling with her hair, hoping someone would notice. Finally, the boy who sat behind her and used to always pull her hair, Eric, leaned forward and tapped her shoulder.

Stacy turned around and smiled, if anyone, Eric was sure to notice her hair. "What?" she asked pleasantly.

Eric seemed rather surprised at her smile, usually Stacy just stared him down. "Um..." Eric stammered, "I didn't want to tell you that I noticed but..."

Stacy smiled even larger, finally, someone had noticed she and Tracy do not look alike anymore.

"But..." Eric continued, Stacy's smile was really making him nervous, "But, Charley McFarley hit you with a spit ball and it's stuck in your hair." Eric ducked his head immediately, as if that would protect him from Stacy's glare. "Oh, by the way," he continued, daring to peek his head up for a minute, "which one are you anyway?"

But Stacy did not hear Eric, she was far too upset to hear anything. She closed her mouth so tight it would take a crowbar to open it.

She did not speak another word for the rest of day. Not one person at school noticed that she had cut her hair. And every single one of them asked "Which one are you?" Of course, since she had vowed to never answer that question again, she could not answer them. And no one would talk to her when they did not know which one she was.

The Twins walked home from school in silence, Stacy was too mad to speak, and Stacy was too mad for Tracy to speak. Stacy stormed into the house, leaving Tracy standing alone in the living room. Stacy stormed back soon enough, holding her severed braid and the Super Santa Glue in her hand.

"Do you want me to glue it back on?" Tracy said before Stacy could get a word out. After all, they were Twins, and Twins always know what the other is thinking, even before the other says it.

Stacy did not say anything, after all, she already knew that Tracy knew the answer. She just pushed the braid and glue into Tracy's hand and turned around.

Tracy fitted the braid to Stacy's now short hair, careful to match all the ends perfectly, naturally she wanted Stacy's hair to be just as even as it was before. Then she applied the Super Santa Glue, making sure she covered every single strand.

"There," Tracy said triumphantly, "Finished."

"Good," Stacy said running her fingers through her now long hair, "If people can't tell us apart no matter what, then I at least want my long hair."

Mrs. Claus

Mrs. Claus

AS you know, the job of "Santa Claus" passes from one member of the Claus family to the next. Each Santa Claus has the post for about twenty years or so, then passes it on to the new Santa Claus. Now a question that I have often been asked, is what happens when a girl is the best choice to be the next Santa Claus? The answer is she becomes Santa Claus. I found in our family album the story of the first girl to become Santa Claus, about 500 years ago. It is about Carolyn Claus, the first Lady Santa Claus, who succeeded her Uncle Frederick, as Santa Claus around the beginning of the sixteenth century, 1502 to be exact.

At a very young age, everyone knew that Carolyn Claus was going to be Santa Claus, she just had that special aura about her that told the rest of the family that she had to be Santa Claus. And what do you know, Carolyn grew up and became the youngest Santa Claus ever.

"What would the children see?" was the question the whole family asked. As you know, everyone sees whatever he expects to see when he looks at Santa Claus. If a child imagines Santa has white hair, then they see a white haired Santa. If their image of Santa Claus is purple with orange hair, that is what they see. But no one knew how a child would see Carolyn. Would they see Santa Claus as a woman or as a man?

Now no one ever considered not letting Carolyn become Santa Claus, she was too perfect for the job. They were just curious as to what the children would see. They had tried hard to release legends about a female Santa Claus, but all turned into stories about a Mrs. Claus. And that was just going to have do, because by this time it was Christmas and Carolyn and the family were already loading the sleigh.

Of course, no one was more curious about how the children would see this Santa Claus, than this Santa Claus herself. This was going to be Carolyn's first Christmas, the first time she would put on the traditional Santa Suit, and naturally the first time anyone was going to see her in it.

Carolyn attempted to experiment with her brother Mathew's children. She got into the suit on Christmas Eve and showed herself to the children.

"You look like Aunt Carolyn," Anne Louise, the youngest, giggled.
The others agreed, giggling as well.

Carolyn sighed, "You mean there's no change at all? Try imagining me with a long white beard and see if it works."

Christopher, Charlene and Anne Louise giggled even more, "You look silly with a beard."

"Can't you try harder?" Carolyn begged.

This threw the children into such a fit of giggling that they were completely useless for the rest of the night. Carolyn gave up and went to her Uncle Frederick who was adjusting the TimeDevice.

"Do I look like a Santa Claus?" she asked.

Her uncle shook his head, "You look like Carolyn."

"That's what the kids said," Carolyn said.

"Well, of course they did," her uncle replied.

"What do you mean?" Carolyn asked, "Aren't children supposed to see Santa Claus exactly more or less as they imagine him?"

"Yes," Uncle Frederick answered, "But Mathew's kids know you and they know you're Santa Claus, and they know I was Santa Claus too. They're not like all the other kids of the world who have to imagine Santa Claus, they see Santa Claus. Do you follow me?"

"More or less," Carolyn answered, more or less was the most anyone could understand her uncle. "So you're saying that I need to find another kid to test this out on. Some kid who's never seen Santa Claus and has to imagine Santa."

"Actually I'm trying to get around to reminding you how to work the TimeDevice," Uncle Frederick said. Her uncle was an inventor and loved to talk about his inventions. In fact he was the inventor of the Santa Claus Bag which is bigger on the inside than on the outside, that is how Santa gets so many gifts on to so small a sleigh. Uncle Frederick had just completed a new upgrade to the TimeDevice.

"I know how to work it," Carolyn said. True to her good nature, she did not roll her eyes. "You've gone over it about a hundred times," Carolyn continued, "and that's just today."

"How about just one more time," Uncle Frederick pleaded, "just to make sure. Please."

Carolyn had to try really hard now not to roll her eyes. She was a good natured person, even better natured than most, but there were only so many lessons on between time travel she could take. Then an idea hit her, "How about we test it out now?" she said, "There's still four hours till Christmas starts, we can go find some kid who's never seen Santa Claus before and test out how I look as well."

"Um..." Uncle Frederick began, "I don't now, that's cutting it awful close to Christmas."

"But we'll be testing out the TimeDevice as well," Carolyn protested, "And we'll be slipping in between time, so we can get back a few minutes after we leave."

"I don't know about that," Uncle Frederick said gnawing on a finger nail.

"You can show me how it works," Carolyn said, if this did not convince him, nothing would, "You can show me exactly how it works in action."

Uncle Frederick did not answer right away, but he was clearly tempted.

"Please," Carolyn begged.

"Oh, all right," Uncle Frederick relented, "Come on," he led the way into the sleigh.

Carolyn went to hook up the reindeer to the harness and then joined her uncle in the sleigh.

Uncle Frederick explained all the buttons of the TimeDevice, excitedly pointing out which ones let you enter between time and which ones let you out again. Carolyn listened with patience until they finally took off.

"Where do you want to go?" Uncle Frederick called over the rushing wind.

"Anywhere," Carolyn answered, "Just long as it's a place where no one has seen Santa Claus."

"How about here," Uncle Frederick pointed down, "Ireland. I don't think we should go very far."

Carolyn nodded, she did not want to work the reindeer too hard before Christmas. They landed easily atop a small log house. Carolyn waved to her uncle and went down the chimney. The family was not asleep quite yet, they were reading, though the youngest children were asleep on the floor. Carolyn hated to ruin the moment, but she was confident they would be happy to see Santa Claus.

The family was not exactly happy when they saw her, they were a bit shocked, but they soon recovered, and then they were happy. Except for the youngest ones who were still asleep and nothing could wake them up now.

Carolyn went over to the oldest child. The child began stammering off his Christmas Wish List at amazing speed.

Carolyn held her finger to her mouth. "It's not Christmas yet," she said, "You have to wait four more hours."

The child looked as though his list just might take four more hours to get through, but he kept his mouth shut for now.

"I just need to know what I look like," Carolyn asked, "Do I look like Santa Claus?"

The child nodded, "You look like Mrs. Claus," he answered.

And that was what Carolyn Claus was known as for the rest of her 37 years as Santa Claus. She was Mrs. Claus, even though it was not entirely accurate at first since Carolyn was a Miss and not a Mrs. But she was good natured enough, as all Santa Clauses are, to let it slide.

The Mighty Quinn Mallory

The Mighty Quinn Mallory

IT is hard to describe The Mighty Quinn Mallory, there are few words one can use, especially for a part Maine Coon cat. But here are the ones you can use — big and fluffy. Mallory is a cat, a particularly large cat, in fact he is larger than small dogs. Mallory is also fluffy, he has long black and white fur which the Twins brush constantly until it fluffs out. He is also a particularly nice cat, he loves it when the Twins hold him like a baby and take him for rides in the baby carriage. This is perhaps how Mallory gained his unusual sense of adventure and mischievous ways.

When the Twins had first found Mallory they had named him Signey Mallory, after a star ship captain they had read about in a book. Unfortunately, Signey Mallory is a girl, and after a few days, the Twins discovered that Mallory was a boy. A name change was in order, so the Twins changed his name to The Mighty Quinn Mallory. Now he is named after an Eskimo in a song.

The Mighty Quinn Mallory lives with me, Laura, The Twins, and Lily the Dalmatian at the edge of a large wilderness area near Snowbird, Utah. Well not exactly on the edge of the wildness but on the edge of a golf course which is on the edge of the Lone Peak Wilderness Area. Cougar, coyote, eagles, hawks, deer, elk, and moose are among the wild animals I have seen from my back porch. I am sure The Mighty Quinn Mallory knows them all.

But even with all the wildness nearby, Mallory never forgot that he had been named after a star ship captain first. And every time the Twins took him for a ride in the baby carriage he imagined he was soaring through space and commanding a fleet of star ships. But after awhile, Mallory wanted a new adventure. He wanted something different from the baby carriage, he wanted a real star ship.

The problem was, where do you get a real star ship? Mallory definitely did not know where to find one, the closest thing to a star ship he knew of was Santa Claus' sleigh. And right then, the idea hit him, he could take a ride on Santa Claus' sleigh. Even though the sleigh never made it to the stars; it at least made it off the ground. The baby carriage only left the ground by accident.

Jonathan Claus

So Mallory decided to stow away on Santa Claus' sleigh one Christmas. He climbed into the sleigh on Christmas Eve when no one was looking, he found a little nook to hide in and he stayed there until the sleigh was loaded and Santa Claus took off. Mallory then climbed to the top of bags of presents to look over the world as they flew. He watched the trees fly by below him. He watched as they passed rivers and lakes. He watched as they flew over mountains and down canyons. All the time, he was imagining he was a star ship captain leading his fleet across the universe.

Every time the sleigh stopped for Santa to deliver presents, Mallory would hide from him under the pile of bags on the sleigh. And every time they took off again, Mallory would climb to the top to watch everything as it flew by.

Now Santa makes a lot of stops when he's delivering presents, so Mallory was spending more of his time waiting than flying. After Santa was about half way finished, Mallory began to get restless. And at one stop, Mallory decided to explore a little, after all, he thought, he had plenty of time to explore while Santa was busy delivering and arranging the toys.

Mallory hopped out of the sleigh, played in the snow on the roof of the house a for little while, looked at some birds in a nearby tree, stared at the stars for awhile. He then decided to go back to the sleigh. Santa would probably be almost done by now. But Mallory could not find the sleigh. He was sure he had left it right there by the chimney, but it was gone. Mallory searched the entire roof, he searched the nearby tree, he searched all of the small garden by the house. There was no sleigh, no Santa Claus, and no way for him to get home.

Mallory sat in the snow and meowed. And for such a large cat, Mallory had an awfully pitiful meow. He sat there all night crying. He wanted to go home now. He wanted his Twins to pick him up and hold him like a baby. He promised himself he would never stow away on Santa's sleigh again. Then Mallory remembered how much fun he had been having on Santa's sleigh before he had gone exploring. So he promised himself if he ever stowed away on Santa's sleigh again, he would never leave it.

In the morning, a little girl found Mallory out sitting in the snow of her garden meowing. She tried petting Mallory, but that did not stop his crying. She even tried picking him up, but he still cried. He wanted his Twins, his home, he even wanted to see his Lily, another one of the

Twins' pets except Lily was a dalmatian not a cat. The little girl tried everything she could to cheer him up, she showed him to her parents and to her brothers and sisters, and they all tried to cheer him up. But Mallory still wanted to go home.

The girl asked everyone she knew if they had lost a cat, but no one had. She tried putting up posters, but no one in her town had lost a black and white cat. Finally, the girl wrote a letter to Santa Claus, after all, Santa had brought her what she had wanted for Christmas, he seemed a very capable person. Santa responded to the letter in no time, he sent the little girl a box, an airplane ticket and the Twins' address in Snowbird, Utah. He told the little girl that Mallory had stowed away on his sleigh, and that he must have lost him at her house. He told her that she could send Mallory back to his home with the Twins.

The little girl was very impressed that Mallory knew Santa Claus personally, so she had her picture taken with him before she sent him traveling back to the Twins.

It took two days for Mallory to get back home, by the fastest means possible, from Sapporo, Japan back to his home with the Twins. And by the time he was back and for many days thereafter, Mallory did not even feel like going outside to his back yard to his golf course wilderness domain. He had had enough of adventures. And now every time the Twins take him for rides in the baby carriage, even though he still imagines he is a star ship captain, Mallory does not wish to get any closer to the stars.

The Age of Reason

The Age of Reason

ONE night as I was reading one of the many Santa Claus diaries stored in the library at the North Pole, I came across this story. Some day I will have to tell you about our library but now let me tell about Santa and René. This story happened during what was called the Age of Reason , in the seventeenth century in the year 1606.

Now during this age, many people wanted to be scientific, and there is nothing wrong with that, the problem is when people want to be logical. You may say there is nothing really wrong with being logical, and you would be right, there is nothing wrong with being logical. The real problem is when you want to stop believing in illogical things. You may ask why is that such a big deal, well I will tell you. When people stop believing in illogical things, Santa Claus is usually the first thing to go. Now, none of you like being ignored, so think about how that makes Santa Claus feel when people say they don't believe in him.

Now the Santa Claus at this time was named Augustus. And Augustus was pretty much just a normal Santa Claus, he liked children and liked toys, and he had the perfect job for someone who likes children and likes toys, delivering toys to children. But Augustus came across something every Santa Claus dreds, a child who did not believe in him. Normally Santa Clauses just ignore the children who do not believe in them, but unfortunately, Augustus could not avoid this one.

The child I am talking about was named René, and he lived in France, in the seventeenth century of course. Now, René was the eldest child in his family, and he took it upon himself to be the logical one of the family. All of his younger brothers and sisters believed in Santa Claus. They thought it was great. Santa Claus would bring them presents and all they had to do was be good, which was not so hard since their parents made them behave themselves without bribing them with presents. But, René had fallen into that problem and was no longer wanting to believe in illogical things. He thought Santa Claus was a very illogical thing. And being the eldest child, René felt it was his duty to make sure all of his younger siblings would be as logical as he.

Jonathan Claus

Of course, none of René's brothers and sisters really cared at all for his logic. As I mentioned earlier, they were quite fond of Santa Claus and the idea of getting presents from him. So try as he may, René could never convince his siblings that Santa Claus was not worth believing in. Which meant that Augustus could never really ignore René, since he had to visit his house every Christmas to give presents to all of René's brothers and sisters, he never left any presents for René because René did not believe in him, and René never noticed for the same reason.

Now at this time, Augustus was fairly new to the job of Santa Claus, and René was really the first child he encountered that really, truly, did not and would not believe in him. Augustus did know of the rule of how Santa Clauses are supposed to deal with children who do not believe, if a child does not believe in Santa Claus, then Santa Claus does not believe in him. I know this sounds like an awfully harsh rule, but you must remember that the child started it, all the child has to do is believe in Santa Claus and Santa will believe in him.

But as I said before, Augustus was rather new to his job, and he could not avoid René because all of René's brothers and sisters were good all year and deserved presents. So Augustus could not help but be concerned about René. And to be honest, Augustus really did not want to just give up on René.

So when Christmas came in 1606, Augustus planned on spending some extra time at René's house. He was planning on performing a sort of experiment, you see, he wanted to know why René refused to believe in him.

Now René was not the only child then that did not believe in Santa Claus, actually there were several, just as there are several now. But Augustus wanted to understand why, he wanted to understand what made these children not want to believe in him. So he decided that René would be his test subject, since René's brothers and sisters were so good. Augustus decided a personal visit from Santa Claus would be just the thing for René.

Augustus was very optimistic that he would be able to change René's mind about Santa Claus. Actually, Augustus was very optimistic about everything, that is why he was even trying to restore René's belief in the magic of Christmas. He spent the entire sleigh ride up to René's house convincing himself that René would believe in him again by tomorrow. And by the time he reached René's house, he was thoroughly sure of himself, purely optimistic, and utterly convinced that René would soon believe in him again.

Augustus landed the sleigh smoothly on the roof of René's house, he gave the reindeer some treats and told them that he would be a bit longer inside than usual. He turned off the TimeDevice. Then Augustus slipped quietly down the chimney with his bag of presents. He took his time sorting out the presents around the Christmas Tree, making sure he made enough noise to wake the children who were sleeping just a little ways down the hall.

After a few minutes of noisily arranging presents, no children woke up to see what was going on. So Augustus, who besides being chronically optimistic was also a little chronically impatient; he took hold of the tree and shook it. The ornaments rang as they clanged against each other, and finally, Augustus was making enough noise to wake up one child. It was René's littlest brother who walked sleepily into the main room. The boy rubbed his eyes, looked up at Augustus, and then he ran right back to the bedroom to wake up all his brothers and sisters.

Augustus could hear the little boy babbling out how Santa Claus was in their largest room setting out their presents, and about how many presents there were. In no time, every child in the house was awake and had come out to see Santa Claus. They all just stood a few feet away from Augustus, looking up at him in awe. Augustus smiled back at them, and looked for René. But René was not there, Augustus even counted the children, but there was definitely no René.

"Where is your brother René?" Augustus finally asked the children.

"He doesn't believe in you," one of the girls answered, "You're really Santa, right?" she asked, suddenly suspicious.

Augustus smiled, "Of course I'm really Santa," he answered.

"René says you should prove it," the girl said.

"Where is René?" Augustus asked, he counted the children again, just to make sure. There was still no René.

"Right here," the girl answered naturally.

Now Augustus was confused. He knew the girl was not lying, she always made the Nice List every year because she never lied. But he could not see René anywhere. "I can't see him," he told the girl, hoping maybe she could explain it to him.

The girl shrugged. "Of course not," she answered, "He doesn't believe in you, and he can't see you either."

"But why can't I see him?" Augustus asked.

"Because if you don't believe in Santa, then Santa doesn't believe in you," the girl quoted her grandfather's often used expression.

Now Augustus frowned, he had been hoping he could change René's mind about believing in him, but apparently he would not be able to do that. If René did not believe in him, then he could not believe in René, even if he wanted to. Augustus sighed, he did not want to give up, but there was nothing he could do for René.

"Don't be sad," the girl said, "It's not your fault."

Augustus forced himself to smile. "Do you want proof that I'm Santa Claus?" he asked.

All the children nodded eagerly.

Augustus grabbed his bag from where he had left it by the fire place. He opened up the bag, showing the children all the multitudes of presents that were inside. The children moved closer and peered in, but none dared get too close, they were afraid they would fall in if they came too close. And Augustus could not blame them for their timidness, after all, as you know, Santa's bag is no ordinary bag, it is bigger on the inside than it is on the outside. And a little child could probably get lost inside it quite easily. Augustus then reached inside and pulled out an extra present for each one of them.

"Does René want one?" Augustus asked, just out of hope that René had somehow seen his proof.

René's sister shook her head. "No," she said, "he says he's too old for toys. Is he too old for toys?"

"No," Augustus answered, "I'm many, many times as old as René, and I still play with toys."

The girl laughed.

"Do you think René will ever change his mind?" Augustus asked, it was just really hard for him to give up on René.

The girl was thoughtful for a moment, then she finally shook her head. "No," she said, "that's just the way René is."

Augustus nodded slowly. René's sister obviously knew him better than he did. If she did not believe he would change, then he most likely would not. Augustus said good-bye to all the children, even to René, though René was not listening. And Augustus finished up delivering the presents, and as he returned to the North Pole, he was starting to reconcile himself to the fact that there were just some people he would not be able to change.

As long as Augustus was Santa Claus, he kept track of René, just hoping he would change. But René never did change his mind, even when he was older and had children of his own, he refused to believe in Santa Claus, because he was too logically minded. Maybe if Augustus had been able to talk to René, if he had been able to convince René that he did exist, then just maybe René might have changed. But René did not believe in Santa Claus, and so Santa Claus could not believe in him.

The Spotted Reindeer

The Spotted Reindeer

LILY thought she was a reindeer. This was not true of course since Lily was really a dalmatian, but Lily still wanted to be a reindeer nonetheless. Lily lives with me, Laura Claus, the Twins and The Mighty Quinn Mallory. My brother, Santa Claus, is always coming over to visit and when he does, Lily always gets to play with the reindeer. Lily loves playing with the reindeer, almost as much as playing with her best friend The Mighty Quinn Mallory.

A little while ago, The Mighty Quinn Mallory thought he was a star ship captain. He stowed away on Santa's sleigh and ended up getting himself lost. Naturally, The Mighty Quinn Mallory told Lily all about his adventure. And now Lily wanted an adventure of her own. Of course, Lily did not want to get lost like Mallory did, she just wanted to fly around with the reindeer while Santa delivered the presents. Lily thought it would be fun, so Lily started imagining that she was a reindeer.

When Christmas started to get near, Lily decided this Christmas she was going to have her adventure. Mallory was still recovering from his own adventure and did not want to go anywhere, especially anywhere that would get him lost thousands of miles away from his Twins. He tried to talk Lily out of it, telling her that she was just going to get lost like he did.

"I won't get lost," Lily barked, "I'm going to stay with the reindeer, I won't wander off like you did."

With that, Lily left Mallory who was lounging comfortably in my chair. Santa Claus was coming for a visit today since it was Christmas Eve and the Claus family always celebrated Christmas early. Of course the Claus Family always celebrated Christmas late as well. Lily had decided to put her plan into action. She was going to dress up as a reindeer, leave with Santa and his reindeer, then fly around with them all Christmas.

Lily found some old fake antlers in the attic, you know, the kind that people use to dress up their dogs with. Lily put the antlers on and looked in the mirror. The antlers looked good, and she looked awfully cute in them, but there was still a problem. Lily, as you know, is a dalmatian, and dalmatians have black spots. The problem was that reindeer do not have any spots, black, white, or purple. Lily looked around for something to cover her spots in, she found a particularly dusty corner of the attic. Lily rolled all in the dust, covering every single spot she had with brown dust. She looked herself over in the mirror again, she looked much better this time, she could hardly recognize herself, she looked so much like a reindeer.

Lily trotted downstairs happily, right past me, right past the Twins, even right past Santa. He was the one you had to look out for, he had much better eyesight than anyone else. Lily trotted right outside to play with the reindeer. Even they did not recognize her. They asked her who she was.

"I'm the new reindeer," Lily answered, trying not to sound like a dog.

"You're kinda small aren't you?" Blixen said looking down at Lily suspiciously.

"No," Lily answered, "It's just an optical illusion. Want to play?"

The reindeer all wanted to play more than they wanted to figure out what an optical illusion was, so they played until Santa was ready to leave. When it was time for Santa, Joy and his family to leave, Lily just got on the sleigh with them. No one noticed in the excitement of all the good-byes.

Flying to the North Pole was even more fun than Lily had thought it would be. It was even better than car rides, and everyone knows how much dalmatians love car rides, except when they have to go to the vet.

In no time at all, Lily was at the North Pole waiting excitedly with the reindeer for Christmas to start. The only problem was that the North Pole was very cold, Lily liked the cold and she loved the snow, but she also loved coming inside and getting under the covers. She really wanted to go in now and get under the covers but that would mean she would not be able to fly around the world with the reindeer. Besides, she reminded herself, Santa would be leaving soon, so she would not be waiting in the cold too long.

And sure enough, Santa came out of his storage shed carrying a couple of large bags of toys followed by Herman Claus, Maya Claus, Michael Claus and Terra Claus all carrying additional bags of gifts. They loaded all nine bags, Santa always carries one bag for each rein-deer. Each bag was a Santa Claus Bag which is bigger on the inside than on the outside so one would have held all the toys but Santa still carried one bag for each reindeer. As the last bag was loaded on the sleigh, Joy Claus, Santa's wife, gave Santa a good bye kiss.

"Everyone thinks elves do the work up here," said Herman, "I never saw an elf who worked this hard," as he hooked Cupid then Comet to the sleigh.

"Aren't you a little small for a reindeer?" said Herman, with a suspicious glance as he hooked Lily next to Comet.

Lily shook her head.

Herman shrugged and gave Lily one more suspicious look before leaving. "All's ready to go," he called to Santa who had already taken his seat in the sleigh.

The reindeer all stomped in excitement and then took off and began their flight around the world. Lily was so excited, flying was so much fun. Then, after something like five minutes in the air, the other reindeer began descending, and Lily did too. Then they stopped at a house, or on top of one, Santa got out, went down the chimney, and left the reindeer to wait for him. Lily waited impatiently for him to come back, she wanted to fly. Santa did not take too long in the house, and soon enough they were in the air again. But far too soon, they landed again, and Santa took care of another house. Lily waited impatiently.

"How long does this take?" Lily asked Comet, who was the harnessed right next to her.

"Days," Comet answered in a bored sort of tone.

"Days!" Lily repeated, "How can it take days? Christmas is only one night."

Comet shrugged, "Santa takes care of that somehow. I just know that it take days, this is really the worst part of the job."

Santa came back, they took off, they landed again, Santa left for another house. They did this again and again and again. Frequently Santa would give them something to eat, but it was always reindeer food. Even though Lily did not mind eating out of the garbage now and again, she did not like deer food. Lily hung her head down between her shoulders, she was cold and tired and wanted to just get under the covers.

When they finally flew over an ocean, the longest flight yet, Lily was too tired to enjoy it. She wanted to go home. When they reached the Southern Hemisphere, where it was too hot instead too cold, Lily noticed the dust was coming off of her fur. Little by little, the dust was beginning to flake right off and Lily noticed in horror that her spots were beginning to show. Lily would have tried desperately to stop the dust from coming off, but there was nothing she could do but wait and watch. Finally all the dust came off and Lily looked like a spotted reindeer.

Jonathan Claus

All the other reindeer were tired by this time and were catching little naps every time they stopped at a house, none of them noticed that Lily's disguise had all but disappeared. Lily kept her head down anyway, trying to hide herself as best she could, but black spots and white fur were not exactly easy to hide among nine reindeer.

"Hello Lily."

Lily jumped guiltily as Santa Claus walked right up to her. He bent down and petted her on the head.

"I see your disguise has finally worn off," Santa said as he petted Lily.

Lily nodded, she felt incredibly guilty for sneaking on this trip now that she was caught.

Santa took the fake antlers off of her head. "You know I can't go flying around with a dalmatian pulling my sleigh. Everyone would expect me to have a dalmatian again next year. And maybe, someone would want me to start using all dalmatians to pull my sleigh and I wouldn't have my reindeer anymore."

Lily nodded, feeling and looking very, very guilty. For those of you who have never seen a guilty dalmatian before, Lily looked approximately ten times more pathetic than a puppy begging at the table. All the other reindeer were just now noticing Lily, which just made Lily feel and look even more guilty.

Santa unhooked her from the harness, "Come on Lily, I can't be seen with a silly dalmatian trying to be reindeer." Santa led Lily up the sleigh where he sat, "You're going to have to sit up here for the rest of Christmas, no more flying."

Lily jumped up to the seat, right next to Santa. She then noticed that Santa had a quilt on his seat. Santa smiled, he knew Lily well. He held up the quilt for Lily who crawled under, and spent the rest of Christmas night under the covers.

Time and Space

Time and Space

NOT many people know how Santa Claus manages to deliver gifts all over the world in one night. Some have theorized that there are many Santa Clauses all over the world. But this is not true, there is only one Santa Claus at any one time. There have been many Santa Clauses throughout history, but only one at a time. And anyway, Santa Claus has the means to deliver presents to the world's population of children by himself. It is not because he moves extra fast, after all, Santa needs time to enjoy those cookies and milk you always leave out for him. No, Santa delivers all the presents in one night by slipping between the fabric of time itself.

Now, this is very difficult to explain, and plus I am not allowed to discuss it in detail. This technology has been the most treasured secret of the Claus family since the third Santa Claus, Socrates Claus who invented the Time Device. And no one is allowed to give it away.

However there is one case in which a Santa Claus gave away part of the secret. It was awhile ago, when my Great-Uncle Jonathan was Santa Claus around the end of the nineteenth century.

This Jonathan Claus was one of those people who is constantly perfecting things, even things you do not think are broken, and constantly telling people about things no one but him really cares about. Uncle Jonathan figured if he had not become Santa Claus he would have a been a teacher or an inventor, or an all around famous, award winning scientist. But he was just as happy with giving out presents to all the world's children and all those who still believed they were children, just the same. In short, Uncle Jonathan was a very pleasant fellow though he did have a tendency to talk your ear off. Especially if you got him started on the family secret, the device that allows Santa Claus to do what Santa Claus has to do.

Uncle Jonathan always wanted someone who would take as much interest in the family secret as he did. But none of the other Clauses at this time were too interested in physics and time and space in general, actually, you usually only get one like Uncle Jonathan once every generation or so. Even Uncle Jonathan's second cousin Alice, who was lined up to take over as Santa Claus when Uncle Jonathan retired was not all that interested in the mechanics of how Santa delivers the presents in one night, just as long as she *could.* So Uncle Jonathan was always on the look out for someone who loved physics and math like he did.

And one Christmas, he found someone.

As you must know, Santa Claus has to spend all year compiling his list of who was naughty and who was nice. But Santa has another list as well, what all the nice children want for Christmas. And then he has a list of what the nice ones *can* have for Christmas, after all, he can not go and deliver a pony to a child who does not have a barn.

So one year as Santa was compiling his list of what the nice children wanted for Christmas, he came across a case that stumped him. A little Jewish boy in Germany said he did not want anything, of course Jewish boys did not normally ask for presents for Christmas, but they are children too and children always want presents. But this boy wanted nothing, nothing at all. Uncle Jonathan checked it twice, he even checked it thrice. The little boy in Germany did not want anything. Uncle Jonathan even double checked to see if the boy had been nice. The boy was not doing very well in school but overall he had been good.

And so, Santa was stumped, he moved on to the next case. And every day until Christmas, Uncle Jonathan would skip over that boy and move to the next, until he had his entire list made up. Except for that one boy. Uncle Jonathan had no idea what to do, so he decided to ask the boy in person. On Christmas night, Uncle Jonathan made sure to set some time aside to have a talk with this little boy in Germany. He packed some extra toys in the sleigh, and set out to deliver the presents.

Now, Uncle Jonathan was slightly nervous about talking to this boy, after all, he had never had a child who did not want anything for Christmas before. And neither had Joshua Claus, his father and predecessor or Marcus Claus his father's predecessor, so Uncle Jonathan had no one to ask advice of. Uncle Jonathan prepared himself for the conversation while delivering gifts around. And then when he finally reached Germany and he finally reached the little boy's house, Uncle Jonathan did not feel prepared at all, but there was no putting it off.

Uncle Jonathan went down the chimney and headed straight for the little boy's room. Being Santa Claus, he knew exactly where it was. He did not have to wake the little boy, the little boy was already awake and looking out his window. He did not even seem surprised when he saw Uncle Jonathan dressed up in the traditional Santa Suit.

"Do you know who I am?" Uncle Jonathan asked the little boy, in German of course since all Santa Clauses are accomplished linguists.

The boy nodded, "Yes, you're Santa Claus."

Uncle Jonathan smiled, "That's right, do you know why I'm here?"

The boy shook his head, "No,"

"I'm here because you didn't tell me what you want for Christmas," Uncle Jonathan explained, "And since you were nice this year, I need to give you something."

"I don't really want anything for Christmas," The boy answered, turning back to the window.

"Oh, come now," Uncle Jonathan said still smiling, "you must want something for Christmas. Don't you like toys?"

The boy shook his head, "No, they're boring."

"Boring!" Uncle Jonathan was quite shocked, he loved toys and always played with them before he had to give them away to the children. "Well, what do you like?" he asked once he had recovered.

The boy shrugged, "I don't know."

"Well, there must be something," Uncle Jonathan said.

"Well..." the boy began.

"Yes," Uncle Jonathan encouraged, "Go on, what do you want?"

"I want to know how you do it," the boy finally answered.

Uncle Jonathan was lost for a minute. "How I do what?" he asked.

"How you deliver all the presents in one night," the boy answered, "Are there more than one of you?"

Uncle Jonathan smiled and shook his head, "No, there's just me."

"Then how can you do it?" the boy asked again, looking up at Uncle Jonathan with a new enthusiasm.

Uncle Jonathan looked down on the boy's eager face. He knew what the boy was asking was a secret, and a well guarded one at that. This was not just something one could go telling children, after all most children would not understand it yet, most adults would not understand, even most of the Claus family would not understand. But there was something about this boy's face, about how eager he was to know, something that told Uncle Jonathan that this boy would understand maybe if he just told him the first part. And he had to give the boy something for Christmas, no Santa can ever skip a nice child. It just was not done.

"All right," Uncle Jonathan said sitting down by the bed near the boy, "I'll tell you, but I can only tell you a little bit, just the beginning."

Jonathan Claus

The boy moved up to edge of the bed, eager to hear more.

And that was the only time Uncle Jonathan ever found someone as enthusiastic about physics and the mathematics of time and space as he was. Years afterwards, he heard that the German boy, Albert Einstein, grew up to be a famous scientist. Of course by the time that happened, Uncle Jonathan had retired to the tropical island all Santa Clauses retire to. But he always remembered that little boy who had let him talk longer about science than any other person had and who had been interested in every single word. And it was the best Christmas present a Santa Claus ever got.

The Lizard and the UFO

The Lizard and the UFO

ONE particularly strange addition to my family is what we call The Lizard. Of course, The Lizard is not an actual lizard, it is just a nickname for my niece, Elizabeth. You know Elizabeth, Lizard Breath. Anyway, The Lizard makes quite an interesting story, though she is even more interesting in person. You see, The Lizard has a few obsessions, mostly the Beatles and Star Wars, but also UFOs. She has never seen a UFO, but that has not stopped her from wanting to see one. Of course, this story does not have any UFOs in it, this is the story of the UFO The Lizard created.

At this time The Lizard was a teenager, and you know what teenagers are like. Helen, my little sister, and Kent certainly knew. You parents who do not know what they are like, you will learn soon enough. At any rate, The Lizard was quite mischievous and inventive. She was always testing the limits and never wanted to do anything the ordinary way. Part of this mischievous nature of hers was playing tricks on people. It was one of The Lizard's favourite pastimes. Of course, most of the tricks she played were on her little brother, Tommy, and needless to say, Tommy was not very fond of this pastime or teenagers in general.

Actually, The Lizard and Tommy hardly ever got along, they were constantly fighting. Except for one day, and one trick, when The Lizard and Tommy combined forces to almost pull off the greatest prank in the history of mankind.

As I said before, The Lizard was always on the look out for UFOs until one day she got tired of this. She decided to make her own UFO. After all, if aliens could do it so could she. The Lizard sat for a moment, trying to think of what she would need to make a UFO. Of course, she would need something that flies, after all, UFOs are Unidentified Flying Objects. She had to find some sort of object that flew and disguise it so it would be unidentified.

As a member of the Claus Family, The Lizard knew what would be perfect. As you may have guessed, The Lizard was thinking of Santa Claus' famous sleigh. True, it was not a saucer shape like most UFOs, but as I mentioned, The Lizard was an inventive teenager. She did not like to do things the normal, ordinary way.

Now what she needed was some way to disguise the sleigh, though most adults may not recognize it, every child in the world would know Santa's sleigh in an instant. The Lizard lay back on her bed thinking about that problem. How to disguise the sleigh. She stared at the florescent green stars she had pasted to her ceiling, thinking about the problem, and then the solution hit her. Florescent green. She would paint the sleigh florescent green, then the normally red sleigh would glow bright green in the dark and still be red in the light. And if that did not make everyone think it was a UFO, then The Lizard just did not know what would. Plus, painting the sleigh would not be too hard for her, she could just visit her Uncle Tomás who is the current Santa Claus. Pretending to be visiting the reindeer for some reindeer games, she could sneak off to the barn where the sleigh was stored and paint it florescent green.

And now came the hard part, flying the sleigh. The Lizard knew she would have to fly soon after she painted it. Santa's sleigh had been red for two hundred years, someone was bound to notice if it suddenly turned up green in the dark. Getting to the sleigh was no problem, even painting the sleigh was no problem. But getting it off the ground, now that was a problem. But that did not stop The Lizard from making her plan anyway, she would not be able to visit Santa until that weekend anyway. She figured she would come up with something by then.

And when that weekend finally came and when The Lizard, and Tommy, and the rest of their family was getting ready for their visit at the North Pole, The Lizard still had no idea how she was going to get the sleigh flying. As it stood, her plan was this:

1) Hide the florescent paint she had bought in her backpack,
2) Tell everybody she was going to play with the reindeer,
3) Sneak into the barn and paint the Sleigh,
4) Fly the sleigh to the Yukon and hide there until dark,
5) Fly the glow-in-the-dark sleigh around the world.

You may be wondering what The Lizard would to do after flying the sleigh around the world. How she planned to get home. How she would remove the florescent green paint. Truth was, The Lizard had not thought that far ahead, she usually did not get that far in her plans. She was usually caught before she ever got to the sixth step of any plan.

But The Lizard still had not thought of any possible way she could get the sleigh in the air without anyone noticing. And now they were almost ready to leave for the North Pole. The Lizard was desperate, she had to be to come up with the solution she came up with. It was the unthinkable, ask for Tommy's help. The Lizard was pretty sure she could get the sleigh to the Yukon if she had a distraction. The problem was, how could she stage a distraction while she was flying the sleigh. The answer, of course, is to have someone else doing the distracting while she was doing the flying. And that answer meant enlisting the help of the Dreaded Little Brother.

The Lizard packed her florescent green paint in her backpack. She even packed her alien mask from Halloween and the tinsel wig I had given her just for good measure. And then she nerved herself for an encounter with Tommy, thinking back, it would be the first time she had initiated a conversation with him in nine years. The last time had been when The Lizard had been six, and Tommy had been two, and she had yelled at him for breaking a toy of hers. The Lizard still missed that toy, and it was painful to have to be asking for help from Tommy, but it had to be done, for the sake of tricks and UFOs, it had to done.

The Lizard paused in front of Tommy's bedroom door, she almost knocked, but then remembered whose room it was. The Lizard burst inside, fortunately she did not interrupt anything important, just Tommy playing the ninth level of some computer game. Tommy was distracted just long enough to lose.

"Nice going Lizard," he said, "Now I have to start again."

The Lizard did not reply. She had not thought out what she was actually going to say to him. She ended up just staring at him.

"What do you want?" Tommy asked, "I didn't take anything out of your room, and the chocolate bars in the freezer were mine anyway."

"No they weren't," The Lizard said outraged, "Those chocolate bars were mine."

"Nuh uh," Tommy said.

"Uh huh," The Lizard argued.

"Nuh uh," Tommy argued back.

They continued like that for a good five minutes, they had that same conversation between three and twelve times a day.

"Those chocolate bars were mine," The Lizard said finally, "I was the one who hid them in the freezer in the first place."

"And I was the one who found them," Tommy said smugly.

The Lizard resisted the urge to wipe that smug look off of his face, physically wipe it off of his face. She reminded herself why she was here. "I'll beat you up later," she said, "right now we have more pressing business."

"Like what?" Tommy asked, he tried not to sound too eager. You see, Tommy actually did like tricks and pranks, he just did not like the ones The Lizard played on him. As previously mentioned, the majority of The Lizard's tricks and pranks were played on him. Of course, this was not entirely because The Lizard was vindictive or mean, it was mostly just lack of targets. They lived on the edge of a small town and Tommy was convenient.

"Like it's none of your business," The Lizard answered, she wanted Tommy to help her, she just did not want to tell him anything.

"Then whatever you want, you can forget it," Tommy said turning back to his computer, "If you don't tell me what your doing, then I won't help you."

"How do you know I want your help?" The Lizard asked, trying to sound as though she did not in fact want his help.

"Why else would you be here?" Tommy said, "You probably have some sort of prank planned out, but you need two people for one part and I'm the only one you can get. And if you don't tell me what you're planning then——"

"Yeah, I know," The Lizard interrupted, "Then you won't help. Well fine, I'll figure out a way to do it alone."

"I was going to say. I'll tell," Tommy finished.

"You can't do that," The Lizard protested, "You don't even know what I'm going to do. You don't have any proof to show Mom or Dad."

"I don't need any," Tommy smirked, again, The Lizard had to resist the urge to physically remove the expression, "I'm sure you've got something in your backpack you're not supposed to have. If I tell on you, they'll check the backpack."

Tommy did have a point, of course, he would not be able to tell anyone if she glued his mouth shut. But, of course, that would not get her anywhere, she would just get in trouble for that, and she would never be left alone long enough to turn Santa's sleigh into a UFO then. So The Lizard controlled herself, and finally relented to Tommy's demands. "All right," she said, "I'll tell you what I'm planning, but you have to help now."

Tommy's smirk was replaced with a grin as he nodded, "Of course I'll help, tell me what you need," he said.

"I'm going to fly Santa's sleigh," said The Lizard, she left out the part about painting it green on purpose, Tommy did not need to know everything, "So I need you to distract everyone so I can get away. Got it?"

Tommy nodded. And at just that moment, their parents came in and told them they were leaving right now for the North Pole. It was a fairly long drive to the North Pole from where they lived. The Lizard and Tommy entertained themselves on the trip by fighting as usual. It would have looked suspicious if they appeared to be getting along, then their parents would have known for sure they were up to something.

The Lizard took Tommy aside once they reached the North Pole. "You know what you have to do?" she asked.

"Yes," he answered, rolling his eyes, "I'll distract everyone while you fly the sleigh."

"Good," she answered, "Give it about half an hour, then start distracting. OK?"

Tommy rolled his eyes once more and nodded. Then The Lizard asked permission to go play with the reindeer.

The first part of her plan had of course worked great, no one suspected that she had florescent green paint in her backpack, they may have suspected she had something, but not florescent green paint. The second part worked great as well, she was given permission to play with the reindeer. Even the third part of her plan worked great, she painted the entire sleigh in less than half an hour. Now the sleigh did not really look much different after its new paint job, it was florescent paint, it would only show up in the dark. But The Lizard had known that, so she was not concerned. And now it was time for the fourth part of her plan, Tommy's distraction.

The Lizard had already hooked all nine reindeer to the harness, she had already taken her seat in the sleigh, she had a good, firm grip on the reins. Once Tommy got everyone distracted, she would take off, fly quickly to the Yukon and then wait for nightfall.

The Lizard heard some shouting outside, she assumed this must be part of Tommy's distraction. She flicked the reins lightly, and the nine reindeer took off. The Lizard smiled to herself, it actually looked like she was going to get away with it. It would be the first time she had ever gotten away with anything.

But The Lizard's smile faded quickly when she discovered that the shouting, which she had supposed was all part of Tommy's distraction, was following her. She looked down and saw everybody, meaning her parents, Uncle Tomás and me, looking and shouting at her. They did not look happy. But they did not look as upset as The Lizard did once she spotted Tommy, who was supposed to be distracting them, pointing straight at her. Santa called the reindeer and they flew down to meet him, there was nothing The Lizard could do to prevent it. The reindeer were very well trained.

The Lizard's parents, naturally, were quite unhappy with her, but even they could not get a word out before The Lizard dragged Tommy aside. "Where was your distraction?" she demanded.

Tommy shrugged. "I did distract them," he protested, "it just didn't last very long," he shrugged again, "I was desperate, so I pointed to the flying sleigh hoping that would distract them."

"You idiot," The Lizard said, "How can you distract them from me by pointing to me?"

Tommy shrugged once more. "Well it worked," he said, "they're distracted."

Tommy was right, The Lizard's parents were very distracted, so distracted they took The Lizard and Tommy home that very moment. And it was Christmas Eve before The Lizard saw Uncle Tomás, Santa Claus again. As usual the family was at my house exchanging gifts. The Lizard was not even allowed to go out with Lily the Dalmatian and The Mighty Quinn Mallory to say hello to the reindeer.

But, of course, that was not quite the end of the UFO prank. You see, as I mentioned before, there is a funny thing about florescent, glow-in-the-dark paints, you can not see them until it is dark. So Santa's sleigh looked red in the daylight, and he always kept it in the barn at night. So, Santa never noticed that his sleigh had been painted, that is, not until Christmas. Even at that, he was never sure it was The Lizard who painted it.

Now, The Lizard was punished appropriately for attempting to fly Santa's sleigh, of course she would have been punished more if her parents had found out she had painted it too. But it was all worth it in The Lizard's mind. The Lizard listened with joy to the radio all that Christmas Night, listening to more UFO sightings being called in than she had ever heard before.

Herman Claus and the Elves

Herman Claus and the Elves

AS everyone knows, Santa Claus delivers toys to children all around the world on Christmas. But what few people know is, Herman Claus, Santa's cousin, makes the toys Santa delivers on Christmas Night. Well, he does not actually make every single toy that gets delivered, but he does design them, well at least all the good ones. Herman is very, very good at his job, and he enjoys it.

In fact, there is only one thing that Herman does not like about his job, and that is the elves. Now, Herman does not work with elves, though he has met a few, because elves do not make Christmas toys, Herman does. What Herman does not like is that all the Christmas books and songs talk about elves making Christmas Presents while none ever mentions who really does all the work. And all the children around the world believe that their Christmas toys are made by elves.

Fortunately, Herman spends most of his time up in the North Pole working on making toys, and never has any children visit him. Except for one year.

A couple of years ago there was this particularly curious child, Esperanza, who just had to know where her Christmas toys had come from. And also, she wanted to meet the elves she thought had made those toys. And so, one Christmas, Esperanza decided to travel all the way to the North Pole to meet the elves. Of course, Esperanza had no idea how she was going to get to the North Pole, and she did not figure out a way to get there until July.

Esperanza had figured out that there were no planes that went to the North Pole and that there were no buses either. It was definitely too far to walk, or ride her bike, since she did not want to be away from home too long. She did not want her parents to worry about her.

But one day in July they were having a Hot Air Balloon show, and Esperanza finally figured out a way to get to the North Pole. Before the Balloons took off, Esperanza hid herself in one under some extra sand bags. She waited until the Balloon's pilot climbed aboard, until he waved good-bye to everyone, until he took off. She waited until they were high enough from the ground before coming out from under the sand bags. Needless to say, the Balloon's pilot was quite surprised and it took him about ten minutes to calm down enough to listen to Esperanza's explanation.

"I *need* to get to the North Pole," Esperanza explained.

"Why?" the Balloon pilot, whose name was Juan Diego, asked, "People don't just *need* to go to the North Pole very often you know."

"But I need to know how my toys are made," Esperanza explained, "And they are made at the North Pole, so I need to go there."

"Your toys are made in a toy factory," Juan Diego said, "Your parents buy them from toy stores and that's where they come from, not the North Pole."

"No," Esperanza answered, after all, she knew a lot more about this than he did obviously, "I'm talking about my Christmas toys, and the ones Santa Claus brings, and Santa Claus is from the North Pole, you know."

"There's no such thing as Santa Claus," Juan Diego said, "I better take you back to the ground now."

"No," Esperanza begged, grabbing hold of Juan Diego's arm before he could reach the controls, "We have to go to the North Pole, don't you want to see the elves?"

"What elves?" Juan Diego asked, trying to shake her off his arm, "I thought you wanted to see Santa Claus, what's this about elves now?"

"Elves make the toys for Santa," Esperanza explained still hanging onto his arm. She was surprised he did not know this, she thought everybody did.

"There's no Santa Claus and there are definitely no elves," Juan Diego said, finally managing to shake her off of his arm, "And we're going back now."

"No," Esperanza cried. Then she resorted to her last option, she had been saving this for last. She looked up at Juan Diego, making her eyes all large, round, and teary. She had been cultivating this expression for years, and it had never failed to work on her dad.

Juan Diego looked down at her, trying to look stern, like he would never give in.

Esperanza made a single tear fall down her cheek. In her experience a single tear always worked the best, if she had more than one, it just looked like she was throwing a fit. "Please," she said as the tear fell off her little chin, "Please take me to see the elves, it won't take long I promise."

Juan Diego's face softened, just a little.

Esperanza made her eyes larger and more pathetic.

"Oh, all right," Juan Diego finally said, obviously not able to take any more, "But we're just going to meet the elves and then go. We won't stay long, got it?"

Esperanza nodded quickly. "Of course not," she agreed, "I just want to meet them."

"Good," Juan Diego said, still trying to appear stern, like he had not really just given in to a little girl's demands.

They flew onward to the North Pole. It was a long way, they passed over mountains, lakes, plains, deserts. Esperanza had known the world was big, she had learned that in school, but she had never known it was this big. And it was taking a lot longer to get to the North Pole than she had thought it would, she was worried that she would not be able to make it home soon enough for her parents not to worry.

Esperanza and Juan Diego finally flew past all the mountains and lakes to where it was all white and covered with snow. Juan Diego looked worried, like he had thought they had flown too far, but Esperanza knew exactly where they were. She had been studying the globe ever since she had decided to go to the North Pole, and on the globe the North Pole was white. She knew they were close, she just had to look out for the toy factory.

"There! There!" Esperanza shouted as she spotted a plume of smoke, "That has to it! That has to be the elves' toy factory!"

"Where?" Juan Diego asked.

"Right there," Esperanza answered, still shouting and still pointing, "Just land right there please."

Juan Diego landed right there as he was told. Esperanza immediately jumped out and ran toward the toy factory. Juan Diego just stood still staring at the great, big toy factory with an odd expression. Esperanza figured he had not really expected to find anything at the North Pole.

Esperanza ran inside, expecting to find rows and rows of elves working diligently on all the toys for next Christmas, after all, she knew they would take all year to make enough toys. But Esperanza did not find rows and rows of elves inside, she did not even find a single elf inside. Instead, she found Herman Claus, all alone hunched in his seat over a table working on some sort of tangled mess of wires and plastic. Now Herman is a very big man, over six feet tall, and like all of the Claus family, he is not thin. There was no way Esperanza could mistake him for an elf. She walked up to him slowly, wondering who this man was and where all the elves were.

"Excuse me," Esperanza asked quietly.

The man was not paying any attention to her as he seemed to be absorbed in his work, grumbling to himself.

"Excuse me," Esperanza said again, "Are you making Christmas toys?"

"Of course," the man said grumpily, not even looking at her, "Do you think I'm working on Easter Eggs?"

"Um... No," Esperanza answered, she had no idea who this man was, and she wanted to see the elves now, "Excuse me, but where are all the elves? Do they only work in winter, or something?"

The man finally looked up from his work; Esperanza saw his snow white hair. She would have surely mistaken him for Santa Claus if he had had a beard. "Elves work in winter!" he exclaimed, "What makes you think any elves would be working here at all?" he demanded.

"Well," Esperanza answered, wringing her hands nervously, "Don't elves have to make all the Christmas toys for Santa?"

"Elves? Make Toys!" the man said grumpily, as he worked on the electrical circuits of what looked like a very complicated toy, "I've never seen a elf work this hard. Never seen an elf work at all, for that matter. They just walk around their forests remarking on the shapes of trees, or some nonsense like that."

"But I thought they made Christmas toys," Esperanza said.

"Of course they don't," the man answered, "I make Christmas toys." The man then turned back to work on his complicated toy.

"Oh," Esperanza said, she would have rather met elves than this fellow, "Who are you?"

The man looked up from his work, clearly annoyed with her, "Herman Claus, Head Toy Designer of the Claus Family," he answered gruffly.

Esperanza's eyes lit up. "Herman Claus," she whispered to herself, "Are you Santa Claus?"

"No," Herman answered, "I'm his cousin."

Esperanza was still impressed with Santa Claus' cousin, after all, she had never seen or met any relatives of Santa Claus before. "And you make all the Christmas toys?" she asked.

"Yes. Well actually I design them," he said gruffly, "Are you disappointed I'm not an elf? Disappointed that there are no elves here, like they say there are in all the books?"

Esperanza thought about it, then shook her head, "I think being Santa Claus' cousin makes up for not being an elf," she answered finally.

Herman then seemed to cheer up slightly, then he quickly returned to his grumpy attitude, after all, he could not go letting people see that he was not really that grumpy, it would ruin his reputation. "So," Herman continued finally, "How do you like your toys?"

"They're perfect," Esperanza answered, "I still play with them."

"I should hope so," Herman snorted, "with all the work I put into them."

Just then, Juan Diego stumbled inside. He stared at Herman for a minute, "Is that an elf?" he asked, "I always thought elves would be a bit smaller, or at least thinner."

Herman did not even bother to answer, he just turned back to his work and said, "Are you done yet?"

"Not yet," Esperanza said, she then leaned closer to Herman's ear and whispered what she wanted for next Christmas.

"You know, your supposed to tell that to Santa," Herman grumbled.

"I know," Esperanza answered, "But I thought you might be able to tell him for me. And invent that toy."

Herman resisted the urge to smile by ducking his head, burying his face back in the toy he was working on.

"OK," Esperanza said turning back to Juan Diego, "We can go now."

Juan Diego looked at Esperanza and then at Herman. "So that's one of the elves that makes Christmas presents?" he asked.

Esperanza nodded, "Yep, only he is not an elf, he's Herman Claus, Santa's cousin," she answered, "I met him so I'm ready to go now."

"Just a minute," Juan Diego said, he quickly ran up to Herman and whispered, "Well cousin Herman, that should take care of the elf stories." You see, Juan Diego was actually a member of the Claus Family. Who else could have flown all the way to the North Pole in a balloon?

He and Esperanza took off in the Balloon and headed for home. Guess what. Esperanza was not even disappointed that Herman was not an elf.

Bags and Bags of Toys

Bags and Bags of Toys

I HAVE already told the story of Carolyn Claus. Now think back to that story and see if you remember Carolyn's uncle, Frederick. Remember, Frederick was once Santa Claus, and he was one of those rare Santa Clauses who loves all the scientific aspects of the job. As you know, the sleigh travels the entire world in a single night using the TimeDevice. The TimeDevice allows Santa Claus to go between time. Santa Claus and his team of reindeer spend hours delivering toys and we see only one second pass.

Well there's another scientific aspect to Santa Claus, and that is how he fits toys for the entire world in his sleigh.

You see, when Frederick Claus first became Santa Claus in 1481, the Santa Claus had to make a lot of trips to deliver all the toys. The Santa Claus would deliver presents to one area of the world. Then he would have to fly all the way back to the North Pole, pick up more toys, and then deliver those to another area. Needless, to say, this was a very time consuming process. Now, it takes my brother a few days in between time to deliver all the presents. Before Frederick invented the Santa Claus Bag, it took weeks in between time to deliver all the presents. It took so much time that Santa Claus had to change teams of reindeer often since they would get so tired.

Now the Claus Family invented the TimeDevice when Socrates Claus was Santa Claus, only the third Santa after Saint Nicholas. Later Frederick Claus, with the help of his friend Leonardo da Vinci, improved the TimeDevice. Since Frederick was so good with scientific problems, it seemed only natural that he would work out some way of fitting more toys into the sleigh.

Well, that is, the idea seemed natural to everybody but Frederick. You see, Frederick was always trying to skim time off of the Christmas delivery schedule by modifying the TimeDevice. He considered that the logical way of handling the problem. He never once thought that he could fix the problem by getting all the toys and gifts on the sleigh at the same time.

There were others who saw that this idea was clearly the way to fix the problem. Who were these others? Well, think of who has the hardest time the longer Santa's delivery takes. Think of who would hate having to fly back to the North Pole every few hours.

That is right. It was the reindeer. Now the only problem the reindeer had was telling this to Frederick. Every Santa Claus is a linguist and speaks many languages but none have ever mastered the reindeer language. The reindeer tried every way they could think of to get Frederick to work on the idea. So one Christmas they tried to communicate with Frederick as best they could.

When Frederick's bags would run out of toys, all the reindeer would sigh at the same time, making it clear that they really, really did not want to fly back to the North Pole. But Frederick petted them and when they reached the North Pole, he gave them treats and snacks.

So then the reindeer tried to be more stubborn. When Frederick and other Clauses finished reloading the sleigh, they all laid down in the snow and refused to get up. So Frederick simply unhooked them from the harness and hooked up a different team of reindeer.

So the reindeer tried being even more stubborn. When Frederick stopped at the last house, all the reindeer laid down and refused to get up again. Frederick asked them to please stand up, but they would not. Then he begged them to stand up and promised them treats. He told them they could rest, but they still refused to stand up. Then, Frederick was reduced to pleading on his knees for them to please stand up and pull the sleigh. Try as they may, no living thing can resist it when Santa Claus pleads for help. So the reindeer gave in. Frederick gave them treats and they all headed back to the North Pole.

The reindeer thought they were making progress when after one Christmas they overheard Frederick talking with his niece Carolyn.

"The reindeer are getting so tired every Christmas," Frederick said, "Sometimes I don't think they can make it.'

"Is there anything you can do to fix it?" Carolyn asked.

"Well, I think I've modified the TimeDevice as much as possible," Frederick answered, "I think Christmas Night for us is as short as it could possibly be."

"Well there must be something you can do?" Carolyn said, "Maybe make a bigger toy bag?"

Frederick was silent for while, obviously thinking very hard about it. The reindeer expected Frederick to come up with the answer they and Carolyn had thought of. Find some way of fitting more toys in the sleigh, then they would have to make fewer trips back to the North Pole.

"I've got just the perfect thing," Frederick announced.

Frederick never explained what the prefect thing was that night, actually the reindeer had to wait until the next Christmas to find out what he was talking about. But they all hoped he had come up with some way of fitting more toys on the sleigh and making less trips back to the North Pole.

That next Christmas, all the reindeer were waiting for Frederick excitedly; by this time they had all convinced themselves that he had come up with the solution. They watched him as he and his family loaded the sleigh, the bags were filled to the brim with toys as usual. The reindeer could not tell if there were any more toys packed inside than normal, but that did not stop them from hoping there were.

They took off from the ground, and the sleigh did not feel any heavier. Then they stopped at the first few houses, the reindeer recognized these houses, they were always the first stops on the Christmas deliveries. The reindeer kept hoping the sleigh would not run out of presents, and then when they reached the usual spot where Frederick ran out of presents, guess what happened? The sleigh ran out of presents. And the reindeer had to fly back to the North Pole to fill the sleigh again.

Now the reindeer were quite discouraged. They forgot entirely that Frederick had said he could fix the problem. That is, they had forgotten until they reached Australia. Now, the reindeer had never really liked Australia, reindeer like the cold and Australia is hot during Christmas Time. In fact, Australia was the reindeer's least favourite place to fly around. But this Christmas, Frederick had something planned.

The reindeer set down in Australia, Frederick got out of the sleigh and unhooked all the reindeer. The reindeer just stood by the sleigh while Frederick left somewhere. They had no idea what was going on, and then, Frederick returned. And he was leading ten kangaroos.

"Now Dasher and Dancer, Prancer and Vixen, Comet and Cupid, Donner and Blixen and Rudolph," said Frederick, "I want you to meet Flossie and Glossie, Racer and Pacer, Reckless and Speckless, Fearless and Peerless, and Ready and Steady."

He hooked the kangaroos to the sleigh and told the reindeer, "Now you can have a long rest, the kangaroos will pull the sleigh for all of Australia."

The reindeer were surprised, but they were happy too. Even though this did not quite solve the problem entirely, at least it did give them a long rest. And the Reindeer thoroughly enjoyed their rest, until Frederick came back to get them and they had to go deliver presents in Europe. While the rest in Australia had helped tremendously, it did not solve the problem, it was still many more weeks of work in between time before Christmas was finally over. And even though Frederick used five different teams of reindeer and two different teams of kangaroos, all were thoroughly exhausted by the end of Christmas Night. They were so exhausted they had to rest all year to regain enough energy for another Christmas.

Now the next Christmas, the reindeer resorted to all their old tricks, sighing, lay down and refusing to move. They even convinced the teams of kangaroos to join in, since after all, flying back and forth from Australia to the North Pole is pretty hard too. And once again Frederick was desperately trying to find a way to help them.

Now right in the middle of that Christmas Night, the reindeer laid down. Frederick pleaded with the reindeer to stand up and pull the sleigh. He promised treats. He promised toys. He promised a long rest at the North Pole. He even promised a change of reindeer teams at the North Pole. All they had to do was stand up and pull the sleigh. The reindeer were ready to give in, as I said before, no one could resist a Santa Claus' pleadings very long. Then all of a sudden, Frederick stopped pleading and he starting thinking.

"We need to go to the North Pole," he said to himself, Frederick was in the habit of talking to himself when he was thinking, "You only lay down when we're at the North Pole, or when we're going to the North Pole. You never refuse to go in between houses."

All the reindeer perked up, was Frederick getting it?

"So..." Frederick chewed on the ends of his mittens, another thing he tended to do when he was thinking, "you must not like the North Pole."

All the reindeer stood at once and tried to shake their heads, which is by no means an easy thing for a reindeer to do. They loved the North Pole, they did not want Frederick to think they wanted to move.

"What's that?" Frederick asked looking down at the reindeer, "You do like the North Pole?"

All the reindeer tried to nod, which was another very difficult thing for a reindeer to do.

"Then why don't you want to go there?" Frederick asked.

The reindeer, of course, could not really answer this. After all, nodding and shaking their heads was hard for them to do, talking was impossible.

But fortunately, Frederick was not entirely slow. True, it had taken him several Christmases to figure out this much, but once he got on the right track, he usually figured things out pretty quick.

"You don't like going to the North Pole," Frederick said to himself, "and you don't like leaving the North Pole." Then it hit him. "Because you don't like having to make so many trips back and forth," he said triumphantly.

Then he remembered what Carolyn had said two Christmases ago, "Maybe make a bigger toy bag?"

"Not a bigger toy bag," exclaimed Frederick startling the reindeer. "A toy bag that is bigger on the inside than it is on the outside. That is what I need."

As soon as Christmas was over, he set to work on designing the famous Santa Claus Bag that is bigger on the inside than on the outside. One bag is so big on the inside that it could hold all the toys and gifts for Christmas. However Frederick and all Santas since his time still carry the traditional nine bags of gifts, one for each reindeer.

And the reindeer, and the kangaroos, are much happier that they no longer have to fly back and forth to the North Pole during Christmas.

The Shopping Mall Santa Claus

The Shopping Mall Santa Claus

NOW here's a question I bet just about everyone is asking right now: if I am really Santa Claus' brother, and if Santa Claus really lives up in the North Pole, then who is that person in the shopping mall? I know just about everyone has gone to the shopping mall around Christmas time and seen someone who looks suspiciously like Santa Claus. Then you waited in line and finally you got to see this Santa Claus and you told him your Christmas Wish List. And now that you're hearing some of the true family stories about Santa Claus, you are beginning to wonder if that Santa who was in the shopping mall was real or not.

Well I'll go ahead and answer that for you, he is not quite Santa Claus, but you still ought to give him your Christmas Wish List because he is a relative of Santa's. You see, Santa can't do all the work himself, and Christmas takes a lot of work. So every year, in November, the Claus Family has a family meeting and we all decide what everybody is going to do to help out for Christmas.

Now my job, of course, is to write this book about my family and to just spread some Christmas Cheer all year round wherever I go. I get off easy, most of my family actually has to work. For example there is my cousin, and therefore Santa Claus' cousin: Alexander. Now one thing you must understand about Alexander is that he really, really looks like Santa Claus. He looks more like Santa Claus than I do. He even looks more like Santa Claus than the current Santa Claus, my brother Tomás. So I am sure you can guess what task is always chosen for him to do on Christmas. That is right, he goes to his local shopping mall, dresses up as his cousin Santa Claus, and there he listens to all the children who come to tell him their Christmas Wish Lists.

Now, Alexander does like his job. Well, he likes his job now, he definitely did not like it when it was first assigned to him. He definitely did not like it at all.

When Alexander was a child he and Herman, who is his brother, used to always help to make toys every Christmas. When they became teenagers, Herman began designing toys and Alexander would help him. And Alexander always thought making toys would be his Christmas job.

But when he was old enough to grow a beard, the family realized he would be perfect for something else entirely.

"A shopping mall!" Alexander exclaimed when he was given the news of what he would be doing this Christmas, "I am not dressing up like Santa Claus for snotty nosed kids in a shopping mall."

"But you're prefect for it," the current Santa Claus said, "You already look like the perfect Santa Claus, and you're not even middle aged yet."

"But I always make toys for Christmas," Alexander argued.

"That was only because you hadn't grown a beard yet," Santa Claus answered, "now that you have, you're far better suited to working as a shopping mall Santa than as a toy maker."

"But... but..." Alexander tried to argue, but he really could not come up with any protest.

"Working in the malls isn't so bad," stated my Uncle Julian, who had been working in shopping malls for a number of years, "You get free cookies at the Cookie Stand and free hot chocolate."

"In Africa we work in the bush. I would like cookies at a shopping mall," said Desmond Claus. Now Desmond had the Claus white hair and the Claus white beard and a dark face. After 1600 years members of the Claus family live in every part of the world, even Tibet.

Now as tempting as free cookies and free hot chocolate were, and they were very, very tempting to Alexander, he was still reluctant to work in the shopping mall. "But..." he argued, "but there's all those kids. I've seen the shopping malls at Christmas time, there's swarms of kids."

"Oh it's not so bad," Uncle Julian said, "Well, it's not so bad when the mall cops manage to get the kids in line. You should've seen one year, it was chaos. There were no lines or anything, just a huge swarm of kids running straight at me." Uncle Julian paused as he recalled the memory, "It was possibly the scariest moment of my life."

"See!" Alexander said, "That's why I don't want to be a mall Santa Claus. I mean, children are all good and fine in small doses but when you get hundreds of them together in the same building, chaos is bound to ensue."

"Oh it only happens about once every five years or so," Uncle Julian said, obviously trying not to make a big deal of it.

But it was enough to scare Alexander away. As you may have guessed, Alexander was slightly afraid of children, and slightly more than slightly afraid of swarms of children. "Why do you need me to work in the shopping mall anyway?" he asked.

"Because it's hard work finding out what every single child in the world wants for Christmas," Santa Claus answered, "Plus I have to figure out who's been naughty and who's been nice, and that takes a lot of time. Sometimes kids that were naughty are nice by the time Christmas comes. And kids are always changing their minds about what they want for Christmas, right up until Christmas Eve. So I need all the help I can get. You'd be surprised how much a few shopping mall Santa Clauses positioned around the world can help. It practically cuts my work in half."

Again, Alexander tried to argue, but he could not really come up with any good, much less convincing, arguments. So he just pouted instead.

"How about this," Santa Claus said, "You work in a shopping mall this year, if you don't like it, you don't have to do it again next year. You can do something else. OK?"

Alexander thought about that. He knew it was a trick, he knew in his family every single deal they made had a catch. He knew Santa Claus was thinking that he would actually end up liking working in a shopping mall. Well, Alexander refused to fall for that trick again. He decided he would go work in a shopping mall this Christmas, but he was not going to enjoy it. He would hate it, then he could prove that Santa Claus had been wrong, and he would never have to work in a shopping mall again.

Well, on Alexander's first day he put on the red and white suit, and went to the shopping mall, determined not to enjoy one single part of his job. He did not even get any free cookies or hot chocolate before starting, after all, he might enjoy that. And soon enough, a long queue of children began.

The first child was brought to Alexander's lap, a four-old girl who was incredibly, impossibly cute. Alexander refused to notice how cute she was, instead he just went ahead and asked, "So, little girl," Alexander used a fairly cheerful voice even though he was determined not be cheerful, he did not want to scare any of the children, "what to you want for Christmas?"

The little girl shrugged. "What do you want for Christmas?" she asked.

Alexander was a little surprised by her question, Uncle Julian had never told him what to do if any children asked questions back. "Um..." he struggled to come up with something to say, "I have to know what you want for Christmas," he said finally, "If you don't tell me, I won't know what to bring you."

"I want to know what you want," the little girl said, "Then I'll tell you what I want."

"Why do want to know what I want?" Alexander asked.

"'Cause I bet I already know what you want," the little girl answered.

"And what is that?" Alexander asked. Now, you must know, that by this time, Alexander was in serious danger of admitting how impossibly cute this little girl was. You see, he was slightly afraid of children, slightly more afraid of swarms of children, but he had no idea how to handle cute children. But he had a suspicion that cute children might just help him get over his fear of the other children. And that was the last thing he wanted, because then he would be stuck with shopping mall duty for the rest of his life. And he would have to admit that Santa Claus had been right all along.

"Milk and cookies!" the little girl said triumphantly, "Everyone knows that's what Santa wants for Christmas."

Alexander smiled, in spite of himself and answered, "Yes, that's right. Now what do you want for Christmas?"

"I want a baby doll and a pony and a puppy," the little girl answered, "and clothes for my baby doll and a toy horsey and a toy kitty, and..."

The little girl's list went on and on, I have to stop there because if I did not the rest of this book would just be filled with her list. But the point was that Alexander was snared, the little girl was cute, he could not help but admit it. And you know what? The child after that was even cuter, and the child after that cuter still. And by the end of the day, Alexander realized that cute kids were not even slightly scary, and that he did not have to be even slightly afraid of them.

And do you know what happened the next Christmas? Alexander was working at the shopping mall again, he could not help himself, because besides not being scary, cute children are addictive. So when Santa Claus was assigning jobs that next Christmas, he simply put Alexander's name down by Uncle Julian's and all the other shopping mall Santas. And Alexander did not argue.

Milk and Cookies

Milk and Cookies

IT has become a bit of a tradition to leave cookies and milk out for Santa Claus. And if you do not do this, you ought to, I personally know just how much Santa loves cookies and milk. I do too. This tradition began some time in the eighteenth century with Nathaniel Claus. Incidentally, it is about this time that the well-rounded, pleasantly plump pictures came into tradition as well.

As you may know, or have at least guessed by now, Santa can not deliver the world's Christmas gifts in one night only. Santa uses the TimeDevice to slip between time, so what seemed like one night to us, is really days to Santa Claus.

Now Santa usually takes a few packed lunches with him, for himself and the reindeer, on Christmas just to keep himself and the reindeer going. Now Nathaniel was quite the fan of sweets, particularly cookies. Every Christmas he would leave the North Pole with an entire cookie jar filled to the brim with cookies. Inside the jar was twice as large as any other cookie jar ever made, so he was able to pack enough cookies for the entire trip.

Nathaniel would snack on his cookies in between stops. One year, Nathaniel had taken a particularly delicious type of cookie with him. This was Theresa's, his daughter's, brand new cookie recipe. Nathaniel was quite fond of them. Theresa was going to be the next Santa Claus, and a Santa Claus who could invent cookie recipes naturally loved children. These cookies were very, very good, you know, so good you could not stop eating them. And Nathaniel definitely could not stop.

He started out just snacking on the cookies between stops, but soon enough, since the cookies were so good, he started carrying the cookie jar inside each house with him as he was setting out the presents.

Well, there came one house that needed an awful lot of presents delivered to it, this family had eight children and every single one of those children had been nice. Nathaniel had to carry all their presents in the house in a bag and since there were so many presents, he had to set down the cookie jar while he arranged the presents under the Christmas Tree. Now, another thing about Nathaniel was he always liked the presents to look nice and neat under the Christmas Tree, or around the table or around the fire place, not everyone in the world has Christmas Trees.

Nathaniel spent more time arranging presents than he did flying. At this house, with so many presents, Nathaniel put a little more effort into arranging the presents than he usually had to. He divided all the presents up into groups of which child received which presents. Then he mixed up the presents, so the children would have to take some time to look for them. And he then made sure that the children would not find the best presents until last.

Nathaniel then looked at the perfectly arranged presents and left. He was quite happy with himself for coming up with an aesthetic arrangement. Or he was happy with himself until he discovered that he had left the cookie jar there. He had set it down to arrange the presents and he had never picked it back up again.

Now, Nathaniel did not realize that the cookie jar was missing until he was quite a ways away from that house. And at that time, since it was over one hundred years ago, the TimeDevice was not as sophisticated as it is today, and Nathaniel could not go back. Santa Claus had a set route, and he could not leave that route or else the TimeDevice would not work properly. Of course, that has been fixed by now.

At any rate, Nathaniel had left behind his favourite cookies, and not to mention, his favourite cookie jar. And he could not go back to get them. Nathaniel had to continue delivering presents to the rest of the world, thinking of his now lost cookie jar the whole time. You see, Nathaniel had to resign himself to the idea that it was lost forever, since he could not go back for it on Christmas Night without messing the TimeDevice up, and he would not be able to go back for it at any other time since he would have to take the sleigh and flying the sleigh at any time other than Christmas always leads to bad things, but that is another story. Anyway, Nathaniel had to assume that his cookies and his cookie jar were gone forever.

Now, at the house where Nathaniel had left the cookie jar, all eight of the children, when they woke up, did not even notice the cookie jar. Nathaniel had left the cookie jar right in the middle of the house's biggest room, but still the children did not even notice. They ran right past the cookie jar and right to the presents. They never even noticed the cookie jar that did not belong there. It was Christmas, and children only look for one thing on Christmas — wrapping paper.

Only after the children had played with all their new toys, and once the parents had tired of their new toys, did the cookie jar finally get noticed. One of the children picked it up, looked it over, reached her hand inside, took a cookie and said, with her mouth full, "When'd we get a new cookie jar?"

Of course no one else in the family understood a single word, since this child was only four years old and her mouth was filled with a cookie.

The child finished her cookie and asked again, "When'd we get a new cookie jar?"

"You didn't get a new cookie jar," the child's older brother answered, "You got a toy horse."

"I know I got a new horse," the four year said defensively, "but I got a new cookie jar too," she held out the cookie jar for her brother to see, "See, it even has cookies in it."

The older brother took the cookie jar, looked it over, and sampled one of the cookies inside, "These are good cookies," he said with his mouth full, so of course no one else understood what he had said.

Eventually every member of the family looked over the cookie jar, and sampled at least one cookie. But, of course, none recognized the cookie jar, they had never seen it before.

"I bet it's Santa's" the four year old decided finally. This answer made perfect sense, no one else could have been in their house on Christmas, so no one else could have left a cookie jar.

The rest of the family agreed with the four year old, that the cookie jar had to be Santa's. Now the problem was how to return the cookie jar to Santa. Santa was not exactly the easiest person to reach, since he lived at the North Pole. But fortunately, the four year old, again, had the answer.

"We can wait till next Christmas," she said, "But we'll all have to be good so he comes."

The rest of the family had to agree with that. And so it was decided, the family would keep Santa's cookie jar until next Christmas, and leave it out for him.

Now, while the family was fully willing to return the cookie jar, they could not return the cookies, since they had eaten all of them before they had known they were Santa's. Since everyone felt rather bad about this, after all, Santa had delivered so many presents and they had eaten his cookies, the family decided to make more cookies for Santa. On the next Christmas Eve, the whole family, except for the youngest who was only two, made cookies and filled up Santa's cookie jar with them. Well, these cookies were not quite as good as the ones Theresa had baked, but they were still very good.

Meanwhile, Nathaniel still missed his cookie jar. Even though he had been without it for a year, he still missed it. The Claus family had given him plenty of other cookie jars, trying to replace the one he lost, but Nathaniel just could not replace that one. It was mostly because the cookie jar Nathaniel had lost was a rather large cookie jar and could fit nearly twice as many cookies in it as any normal cookie jar. But it was also partly because he had had that cookie jar for a long time, and it was red and matched the sleigh perfectly.

Nathaniel was so sad after losing the cookie jar, that the next Christmas, he did not even take any cookies with him. He just flew from house to house without snacking in between.

Then, Nathaniel came to the house where he had lost the cookie jar a year earlier. Nathaniel did not recognize the house, since the family had repainted it a new colour. You can just imagine his surprise at finding his long lost cookie jar, the one he had thought was lost forever, waiting for him in the middle of the house's largest room.

At first, Nathaniel did not believe it was real, he rubbed his eyes, he pinched himself, and it was still there. He approached it slowly, then took off the lid slowly, and then he sampled one of the cookies inside. He was so happy to have his cookie jar back, that he did not even notice that it was filled with different cookies. Beside the jar was a large glass of milk, the perfect companion for cookies.

Nathaniel left extra presents at that house that Christmas. And when the children were explaining to their friends why they had so many presents, they said it was because they left cookies and milk out for Santa Claus. And every other child, hoping to get some more presents out of Santa, began leaving cookies and milk out for him too. Nathaniel was quite happy with this tradition, since it meant he no longer had to carry his own cookies with him and put his cookie jar in danger.

He also left extra presents for those children who set out milk and cookies for him. And the current Santa does too.

Note to Parents

NEVER be afraid to read aloud to your children. They love it. Never worry about how well you read, you are their mother, father, or both. They never remember your mistakes only the time together in magic lands.

I know this from experience. The Twins (they appear in many of the tales) and their older brother were read aloud to from the time they were infants. When each was around five years old, Laura and I read aloud to them J. R. R. Tolkien's *Lord of the Rings* trilogy. It took nearly a year. As adults they remember the story and remember the time together. They do not remember the great difficulty I had with all the strange words and names Tolkien used.

Time was spent during each reading session answering their questions. "What does this word mean?" "Who is this person?" and many other questions only a five year old mind can conceive. Remember the young mind is a growing mind and must ask questions.

The best gauge of future success of a person is how well they can read. A person who can read can learn many new things in any field. The person who loves to read, reads well. The children who were read to and who watched their parents read develop the love of reading.

So take your child on your lap, all those from 1 day to 18 years old, and read a book with them. And if you don't understand my stories ask a child.

Note: This book was type set in a larger than normal type face so your child can see the words while in your lap or next to you.